"Mick invites me to church every week. When we clear up this newest case, I'm going to surprise him and go," Drew said.

Rissa beamed in his direction. "That will make me very happy." She stood and started toward him. He met her halfway, and she gave him both of her hands.

He pulled her into a brief embrace, and Rissa relaxed and enjoyed the closeness of him. Being held in his arms made her feel secure and safe. It was the kind of caress she would have given to anyone who had rededicated his life to God. But she knew it signaled something more. She not only found security in Drew's arms, but peace as well. Was she ready for what was developing between them?

* * *

Books by Irene Brand

Love Inspired Suspense

Yuletide Peril #12
Yuletide Stalker #33
The Sound of Secrets #48

Love Inspired

Child of Her Heart #19
Heiress #37
To Love and Honor #49
A Groom To Come Home To #70
Tender Love #95
The Test of Love #114
Autumn's Awakening #129
Summer's Promise #148
*Love at Last #190

*The Mellow Years

**Song of Her Heart* #200
**The Christmas
 Children* #234
**Second Chance
 at Love* #244
*A Family for
 Christmas* #278
"The Gift of Family"
**Listen to Your Heart* #280
Snowbound Holiday #322
*A Husband for
 All Seasons* #382

IRENE BRAND

Writing has been a lifelong interest of this author, who says that she started her first novel when she was eleven years old and hasn't finished it yet. However, since 1984 she's published more than thirty contemporary and historical novels and three nonfiction titles. She started writing professionally in 1977 after she completed her master's degree in history at Marshall University. Irene taught in secondary public schools for twenty-three years, but retired in 1989 to devote herself to writing.

Consistent involvement in the activities of her local church has been a source of inspiration for Irene's work. Traveling with her husband, Rod, to all fifty states and to thirty-two foreign countries has also inspired her writing. Irene is grateful to the many readers who have written to say that her inspiring stories and compelling portrayals of characters with strong faith have made a positive impression on their lives. You can write to her at P.O. Box 2770, Southside, WV 25187 or visit her Web site at www.irenebrand.com.

IRENE BRAND
The Sound of Secrets

Steeple Hill®

Published by Steeple Hill Books™

Special thanks and acknowledgment are given to
Irene Brand for her contribution to
THE SECRETS OF STONELEY miniseries.

STEEPLE HILL BOOKS

Steeple
Hill®

ISBN-13: 978-0-373-44238-6
ISBN-10:   0-373-44238-6

THE SOUND OF SECRETS

Copyright © 2007 by Harlequin Books S.A.

www.SteepleHill.com

Printed in U.S.A.

"Because thou hast made the Lord, which is my refuge, even the most High, thy habitation; there shall no evil befall thee, neither shall any plague come nigh thy dwelling. For he shall give his angels charge over thee, to keep thee in all thy ways. They shall bear thee up in their hands, lest thou dash thy foot against a stone."
—*Psalms* 91:9–12

I want to dedicate this book to the five
other authors with whom I've worked on
THE SECRETS OF STONELEY
continuity series—Lynn Bulock, Shirlee McCoy,
Lenora Worth, Terri Reed and Valerie Hansen.
It's been a pleasure to work with them.

PROLOGUE

Illuminated by the faint light of a half moon, Blanchard Manor resembled a phantom house. Swept inland by a brisk wind from the turbulent Atlantic, thick fog shrouded the stately mansion with wispy white tendrils. The faint scent of seaweed blended with the pungent fragrance of spruce trees. It was a peaceful night and quietness reigned on the promontory. Presumably the inhabitants of the mansion had long since gone to bed.

A man stealthily opened a side door of the mansion. He paused briefly to survey the moonlit scene before he strode purposefully toward the gazebo at the edge of the manicured lawn. Stopping once, he looked upward at the house, wondering if his daughters were sleeping. He climbed the steps into the gazebo, questioning how long he would have to wait. *Not long,* he thought. His expected visitor wouldn't be late when her financial future hung in the balance.

A figure, swathed in a hooded raincoat, approached the gazebo and hesitated in the shadow of an ancient, sprawling maple tree before entering the small, wooden structure. Soon the wheedling tones of the woman were muffled by the man's strident, angry voice.

The argument intensified, and two faces appeared at a window in the mansion. Kneeling with their arms folded on the sill, the sisters strained their eyes to discover the identity of their father's mysterious visitor. Finally, Ronald Blanchard's voice rang out loud and clear in the stillness of the night.

"If you ever darken my doorstep again, I'll have you killed."

A shaft of moonlight swept across the lawn and highlighted the figure of a tall, powerfully built man with his hand lifted as though to strike the woman. Was he holding a knife? A cloud covered the moon and the gazebo was again plunged into darkness.

The man stormed angrily across the lawn and disappeared into the house, but what had happened to the visitor? A door slammed downstairs, leaving the two sisters alarmed and troubled. They returned to their beds, but not to sleep. Would there ever be an end to the troubles that plagued the Blanchard family?

ONE

With misgiving, Nerissa Blanchard strapped two bags on the luggage carrier and looked longingly around her trendy apartment. How she dreaded the upcoming visit to her family's home in Stoneley, Maine! It wasn't as if she'd been away for a long time. She *had* made two quick trips to Blanchard Manor in the past two months.

Since moving to New York City four years ago, the days that Rissa spent away from the exciting metropolis felt as barren as if she'd been stranded on a desert island. And this trip was also unwelcome because Rissa definitely didn't want to be involved in her twin's wedding.

But what else could she do? Portia had called a few days ago and insisted that she needed Rissa's help to complete her wedding plans.

She couldn't disappoint her sister—they had always been inseparable, and now she would be sharing her twin with Stoneley Police detective Mick Campbell. Rissa hadn't gotten used to the idea yet, but she wanted her twin to be happily married. Drew Lancaster, Mick's sometimes partner, a man she preferred to steer clear of, was her real reason for avoiding the wedding. However, she was determined to be Portia's maid of honor in spite of the fact that Drew would be Mick's best man.

She had only met Drew once—no more than a few hours during her last visit to Maine—so why did thoughts of the man infiltrate many of her waking hours as well as her dreams? Rissa couldn't understand. No one was less likely to fit into her life than a small-town cop without a literary thought in his head. Wrapped up in her career, especially the new play she was writing, she had almost succeeded in putting Drew out of her mind. If only Portia's fiancé hadn't picked Drew to be in the wedding party!

Rissa begrudged every minute she had to spend away from the city, but she and Portia had always been there for each other. There was no way she could refuse to help her twin plan the biggest day of her life.

As she finished dressing, Rissa put aside her personal problems and considered the latest news from home— another reason she dreaded going to Stoneley. She had believed all of her life that their mother, Trudy, had died in an automobile accident when the twins were only three. But their father had finally admitted to faking his wife's death to spare his daughters the grief of knowing that their mother had sunk into a severe case of postpartum depression following the birth of their youngest sister. This new development in the family's dysfunctional history was almost more than Rissa could bear, especially since their mother had escaped from the mental institution almost eight months ago. No one had heard from her since then.

Rissa took a last look in the mirror, satisfied with her appearance. She loved the old-world feel of her newest outfit—a long, black velvet tuxedo jacket and pants complemented by a frilly, open-necked white cotton blouse. She put on a pair of black-and-white leather-and-suede flats and pulled her long, curly black hair behind her left ear, fastening it securely with a silver clip.

Hoping that the newest family revelation would be handled by the time she arrived at her Maine home, Rissa locked the door behind her and took an elevator to the parking area in the basement. She ran her hands approvingly along the side of the sleek, navy-blue Porsche that she'd bought over a year ago. Except for Portia, who never questioned anything Rissa did, the family hadn't hesitated to give an opinion that she was foolish to spend so much money on a car that she seldom used. No one knew better than Rissa that getting around in the city was best done by subway, but when she wanted to go outside the city, she liked the freedom of owning her own car.

Hoping she wouldn't have to be away more than a week, Rissa pulled out of the garage and began her journey. Because she preferred to travel at night, long after rush hour, once on the interstate, the trip to Stoneley would pass quickly. After she started northeast and was out of the heaviest city traffic, Rissa inserted a CD containing the theme music of her off-Broadway play, *Memories of the Past,* which had become a smash hit. The miles passed quickly as she listened to the musical scores and plotted her next play.

Daylight found Rissa within fifty miles of her destination, and she reveled in the beauty of the quiet countryside. A misty sunrise highlighted the villages where powerboats were leaving secluded harbors for the turbulent fishing waters of the Atlantic. A solid mass of spruce trees crowned the bluffs to the west. When she passed through marshlands, black ducks and green herons took wing at her approach.

In spite of her love for the city, a thrill of pride in her native state swelled in Rissa's heart. The coast of Maine was rugged, powerful and breathtaking. God must have given an extra portion of His time to this area when He created the world.

Rissa hadn't told her family that she was making a night drive to Stoneley, so when she was within twenty miles of home, she pulled into a rest stop to call them. Her oldest sister, Miranda, answered the phone.

"Good morning," Rissa said. "I'll be home in a half hour. You can warn Andre that I haven't had any breakfast!"

"Rissa! You surely didn't drive all that way alone, and at *night!* It isn't safe," Miranda said, giving her usual unsolicited advice—as she always did—to her younger siblings.

"But I made it!"

She had expected a long lecture on the subject, but Miranda said, "We haven't had breakfast yet. Something terrible happened here last night. Be careful!"

Rissa held the phone away from her ear. Miranda had hung up on her! What could possibly be wrong at Blanchard Manor to cause her always socially correct sister to be rude? She had hoped that this short visit would be more peaceful than previous ones, such as when her family had been under suspicion in the murder of Garrett McGraw, a private detective her sister Bianca had hired to learn about their mother's death. Sensing that wouldn't be the case, Rissa sighed, joined the flow of traffic on the highway and headed for home.

Despite the sadness that had infiltrated the house as long as Rissa could remember, her heart swelled when Blanchard Manor came into view. She gazed fondly upward at the huge stone mansion with its castlelike facade, though she dreaded what new trouble had descended upon the Blanchard family.

Rissa punched in the security code at the gate and started toward the house.

Aunt Winnie, her father's sister—the only *mother* Rissa could remember—never failed to be standing on the small porch, waiting expectantly when she returned home. Aunt Winnie *was* waiting, but she wasn't her neat, usual self. She still wore her pajamas and robe, and her hair obviously hadn't been combed since she'd gotten out of bed.

Instead of driving to the six-car garage at the side of the house, Rissa swung her Porsche into the circular drive and stopped abruptly. Leaving the door ajar, she ran toward her aunt as Miranda and Portia stepped into view, leaving the huge, wooden stained-glass door open.

"What's happened?" she asked.

"Come inside, dear," Winnie said as she leaned

forward to kiss Rissa's cheek. Rissa's shoes clacked noisily on the marble-floored foyer. Inside the spacious hallway, her eyes were drawn toward the walnut staircase supported by heavy, ornate balustrades—a sight that had welcomed visitors to Blanchard Manor for years.

With an anxious glance at Ronald's office, Winnie motioned toward the room to the right of the hallway.

"Let's go to the living room," she murmured, and they walked quietly into the room that hadn't changed much in appearance since Rissa could remember.

Her sisters and Aunt Winnie sat on the twin settees grouped around a large coffee table.

"What's happened?" she repeated when the door closed behind them.

Winnie motioned for Rissa to sit beside her.

"I've been sitting all night," Rissa said, leaning against the closed door. "I'll stand for a while. Don't keep me in suspense—what's wrong?"

"There was a terrible scene in the gazebo last night," Miranda said.

"Terrible? What do you mean? Has someone else been killed?" Rissa demanded, irritated that they seemed to be beating around the bush.

"I don't think so," Portia answered. "We couldn't see in the dark, but I checked as soon as daylight came. There wasn't a body in the gazebo. The woman must have gotten away."

"It happened about midnight," Winnie said. "Ronald was in the gazebo with a woman. He shouted at the top of his lungs and woke the entire household. There must have been a terrible argument. I don't suppose anybody slept after that."

"Another woman? What's happened to Alannah, his latest flame?"

With a disgusted sniff, Miranda said, "Oh, she's still around, unfortunately. This definitely wasn't a romantic tryst."

"That's right. He threatened the woman's life if she shows up here again," Portia said. "Father didn't come upstairs after that, but spent the night in his office."

A disturbing thought popped into Rissa's head and fearful images built in her mind. "But he *is* all right, isn't he?" she asked hesitantly.

"I've listened at the keyhole a few times," Miranda answered. "He's muttering and pacing the floor like a madman, and it sounds like he's kicking the furniture when it's in his way."

Was her father deranged, too? Her mother had experienced serious postpartum depression. Now that Rissa's psychiatrist had prescribed an antidepressant for her, Rissa feared that she had inherited her mother's instability.

What if her father's mind was also unbalanced? Dr. Pearson, her psychiatrist, had assured Rissa that she had only a mild case of clinical depression and had prescribed a low dose of antidepressants to combat her symptoms. But recalling some of Ronald's temper displays, and his uncaring attitude toward his six daughters, she wondered if her condition was worse than the psychiatrist had diagnosed. And her grandfather,

Howard, had Alzheimer's. What chance did she have against such odds? Would she eventually lose her mind?

Rissa had chosen a Christian psychiatrist, one who counseled her patients with Biblical teachings along with traditional treatment. During the therapy sessions, Rissa often felt as if she were a child again in her Sunday school class at Unity Christian Church. Upon Dr. Pearson's advice, Rissa had memorized a few Bible verses that she called to mind anytime she became depressed. The doctor had insisted that a daily dose of Scripture would be an added benefit to her medication.

Rissa suddenly realized that her aunt had spoken to her twice and that her sisters were staring at her in concern. She forced a slight laugh.

"Sorry! I've had a long night. What did you say?"

"We waited to have breakfast with you," Aunt Winnie said. "Are you ready to eat?"

"Sure. Give me a minute to run upstairs and freshen up."

"I'll bring your luggage," Portia said.

"Put it in our bedroom. I'll wash my hands and face and then join everyone in the dining room."

During breakfast Rissa forced an upbeat manner as she chatted with her aunt and sisters, answering their questions about the success of *Memories of the Past*.

"We saw a glowing review in the local paper," Miranda said. "'Hometown Girl Makes a Splash in the Big Apple.' If an article makes it into our paper, you can be assured that the news has spread nationwide."

"I *am* pleased with public reception to my play," Rissa said, smothering a yawn. "My agent encouraged me to start working on another one right away, so I've been busy writing a new one."

"Now that Portia will be moving back to Stoneley, won't you be lonesome in the big city?" Aunt Winnie asked. "Why don't you come home? Seems to me you could write as well here as in New York."

"I could never be lonely in New York. It *is* my home now," Rissa said. "Coming to Stoneley seems like the end of the world. I can't imagine anything that would entice me to live here again."

"It isn't a good thing to forget your roots," Miranda scolded, and Rissa knew she had sounded a little supercilious. She didn't mean to be that way and decided she would have to work on her attitude. But her relatives who had never lived in the city couldn't understand how life on the fast track *had* changed her priorities.

Missing her youngest sister, Rissa asked, "Has Juliet already gone to work this morning?"

"She's in Florida on a business trip and will be gone for a week or two," Winnie explained.

"Tough luck," Rissa said, with a humorous uplift of her carefully tweaked brows. "Having to leave Maine for a trip to Florida this time of year must have been a *real* sacrifice."

"Well, it was in a way," Portia said. "She didn't want to leave her boyfriend behind."

Rissa had been introduced to Brandon De Witte, whom Juliet had met recently. It must have been love at first sight because the romance seemed to be moving forward rapidly.

After breakfast Rissa took a shower, went to bed and slept until noon. When she was awakened by a knock on the door by her aunt, who announced that lunch was ready, she dressed hurriedly in black silk pants and a hot-pink long-sleeved blouse. A pair of metallic leather flat shoes completed her outfit. She brushed her hair over her shoulders and went downstairs to the news that her father had finally come out of his office, gone to his bedroom, dressed and left for his job as the steel-hearted CEO of Blanchard Fabrics. The women ate lunch alone.

"Do you suppose I can see Grandfather this afternoon?" Rissa asked as they finished the light lunch of crab soup, raw vegetables and cherry torte.

"According to Peg, he isn't having a good day," Miranda said. "She said she would let you know when he's lucid."

"I don't know what we would do without Peg," Rissa said of the sweet-natured nurse who took care of their grandfather round the clock. "Does she ever take a day off?"

"I could count on one hand the time she's been away from the house during the past five years," Winnie said. "But it's her fault—we've tried to get her to take more time off. She says she doesn't know what else she would do."

"She doesn't have any family in this area at all," Miranda said. "She specializes in long-term care and lives in the homes of the families she helps. She apparently doesn't have a place of her own."

"Well, we're fortunate to have her," Rissa said.

When Winnie rang for the maids to clear the table,

Rissa said, "I need a walk along the seawall. Portia, why don't you walk with me to the bluffs? After all, the main reason I'm here is to help plan your wedding. We can make plans as we walk."

"You can't go walking in those clothes," Miranda said, casting a disdainful eye at the garments that had set Rissa back several hundred dollars. "This isn't New York City. You'd better take off that fancy outfit and dress for the weather up here. Remember, it's still April, and you know that we often have snow this time of year."

Rissa winced a little at the censure in her sister's voice. Miranda didn't understand that in this house, she had to have something tangible, like her city clothes, to remind her that there was another life waiting for her.

"Snow! Don't tell me it's going to snow."

"No," Portia said. "The weather forecast is for thunderstorms, but it's still cold outside." Turning to Miranda, she continued, "I'm sure she didn't intend to walk in those clothes," taking up for her twin as she always did. "Our heavy coats and boots are in the hall closet upstairs, sis. I'll go get them."

The twins rarely wore matching clothes anymore, but when they left the house in the jackets they had worn when they'd been teenagers, they looked like two peas in a pod. Although the calendar said it was April, and bright sunshine blanketed the estate, the brisk wind from the ocean reminded them that winter hadn't given up yet.

Portia shuddered when they walked past the gazebo. "I thought Father had killed someone here last night. Who could he be threatening?"

"A better question is 'Who's threatening him?' Most of the time, he's a stranger to me. I often feel as if we not only grew up without a mother but without a father, too. He never has any time for us."

"Or for anyone except his latest paramour." Portia sighed. "He's still dating Alannah Stafford, and I don't think she has any intention of letting him go."

"I'd hoped he had dumped her by now. But let's forget unpleasant things. Let's talk about that wonderful fiancé of yours."

"He *is* wonderful! If anyone had told me six months ago that I would be in love and looking forward to not only having a husband but a daughter, too, I wouldn't have believed them. After breaking up with Tad, I didn't think I would ever trust another man, but Mick is so good for me, and I love Kaitlyn, too. I've always wanted a family of my own."

"Well, you must have gotten all of the maternal genes. I can't imagine myself being a mother. I like little kids, although I haven't seen one yet that I wanted to take home with me. But I'm happy for you. When's the wedding?"

"We haven't set a date yet. We're planning a small church wedding with just three attendants. Kaitlyn wants to be a flower girl, and of course you'll be my maid of honor. As I told you, Mick asked his friend, Drew Lancaster, to be the best man. You remember Drew, don't you?"

Staring straight ahead so Portia wouldn't detect that she had more than a casual interest in Drew, Rissa said,

"Yes, I met him during the investigation into Garrett McGraw's death."

A frigid gust of wind staggered the sisters as they walked arm in arm. Rissa had grown accustomed to a slightly milder climate and the strong blast chilled her to the bone.

Portia seemed less daunted by the strong gale, and she continued, "I wanted your help in choosing the dresses we'll wear. We've never had the same tastes, and I need your input. We'll have to shop in Portland— there are no bridal shops in Stoneley."

"The logical thing would have been for you to come to the city to shop for your bridal attire. There won't be as much choice up here."

"I know, but Mick wants to keep the wedding simple. He's a little put-off with the Blanchard wealth and social standing anyway, and I don't want him intimidated by an expensive wedding. Detectives make a good salary, but he has a daughter to care for...and kids are expensive."

"And where will you live?"

"Mick has an adorable little cottage overlooking the ocean. It's small, but he's adding another bedroom and a bathroom for us." Portia looked quickly at her twin. "I've wondered if I'm leaving you in the lurch since I won't be paying my share of the rent. You like the apartment so much—I hope you won't have to give it up."

"Don't worry about that. The profits from my show will easily make up for your share of the rent."

A tremor in her voice, Portia said, "It's hard for me to imagine that you and I won't be living together anymore. We've always been inseparable. Now I'll be staying in Maine with a husband and a daughter, and you'll be in New York by yourself. I wish you'd move back to Maine."

Although Rissa had been having similar thoughts about being separated from Portia, she laughed nonchalantly. "Do you think I could ever be happy in Stoneley again? There probably aren't more than a half dozen people in this area who have even seen a Broadway show, let alone have any idea of what it takes to write and produce one." She shook her head, realizing that she sounded pretentious again. "I'll miss being with you, sweetie. But you and I have to go our separate ways now. I need to be around people who understand me and my purpose in life."

"I know! But it will be different," Portia murmured.

"*Very* different! While I was driving last night I got a little nostalgic. I remembered so many things about us. Being a twin is wonderful. When we were little, I never bothered with a mirror. If I wanted to know what I looked like, I looked at you. And do you remember the time I wanted a new hairstyle, and while you were asleep, I cut your hair to see how I would look with short hair?"

"Do I remember? That's the first time we ever had a fight. And I thought Aunt Winnie was going to spank you." They both giggled remembering the experience.

With a grimace, Rissa said, "Instead of spanking me, she cut *my* hair, and she didn't know any more about styling hair than I did. After I saw what you looked like, I'd made up my mind I didn't want short hair, but

I got it, anyway. Even now, I dread going for a trim—
I'm afraid I'll hate it like I did my first haircut." They
both giggled.

"And I never had any trouble buying a gift for you—
I just bought something I liked."

"But we didn't always choose the same kind of
clothes," Rissa commented.

"That's because we're not entirely identical—we are
separate people."

"Well, it's been a great ride while it lasted."

"Oh, don't talk like it's all in the past, sis. Surely
we'll have more fun times together."

"Count on it!" Rissa agreed. "I'll leave your room in
the apartment the way it is now—mess and all," she
added with a grin because Portia's room was always
cluttered. By contrast, in Rissa's bedroom, everything
had its place. "It will be ready whenever you want to
bring your family to visit."

They came to the end of the cliff walk. "Let's go back
through the spruce forest," Portia said. They turned to
cross Bay View Road but paused when they saw a police
cruiser approaching.

"Well, well!" Rissa said with a teasing glance at her
sister. "Here comes that wonderful man now."

Portia shook her head. "That isn't Mick. It's his
partner, Drew."

The large cruiser slid to a halt and the window
lowered before Rissa got control of her emotions.

"Hello, ladies," Drew said in a deep-timbered,
composed voice that Rissa remembered all too well. He

was ruggedly handsome with short, chestnut-brown hair and assessing dark eyes that were presently flickering with amusement. "I think I need to visit an optometrist—I'm seeing double."

Bending forward until her eyes were on a level with his, Portia said, "Oh, you tease. This is my sister, Rissa."

"It's great to see you again, Rissa."

"Same here," Rissa replied evenly, having regained her composure. "I understand we'll have the responsibility of keeping the bride and groom cool, calm and collected during their wedding."

"So I've been told, but who's going to keep *us* from being nervous?"

"We'll have to lean on each other," Rissa answered, irritated because she was enjoying this good-natured bantering. But her smile faded when she thought about Drew's small-town position—he could never be husband material. Like oil and water—city and small town wouldn't mix. She was determined to put him out of her mind.

"What are you doing out here?" Portia asked. "Not on official business, I hope."

"Actually I am. We had an anonymous tip about an altercation between a man and a woman here in the gazebo last night. The message came from a cell phone and we couldn't trace the call. Mick was busy on another case so he sent me to investigate. What do you know about it?"

Rissa cleared her throat and pulled on her left earlobe, one of their secret communication codes. Portia looked at her quickly, having gotten the message that she shouldn't give out any information.

"Nothing happened that should concern the cops," Portia said. "Just a family matter—and I'm sure that Father wouldn't want any publicity about it. He's seen about all the police and reporters he wants to during the past few months."

"Well, I'll take a look anyway, if you don't mind. Is the gate locked?"

"No, it shouldn't be. During the daytime, it's usually open for the help and delivery service to come and go," Rissa said.

Putting the cruiser into motion, Drew said, "Enjoy your walk."

He had intercepted the secret message that passed between the two women. Mick had mentioned that the twins were super close. He hoped his buddy wasn't making a mistake marrying a twin who might keep secrets from her husband. Not that Drew was in the market for a wife, but he didn't think he would want to marry a woman who was identical in appearance to her sister, even if she were as pretty as Rissa. And considering the shady circumstances involving the Blanchards now, he had better steer clear of any personal involvement with any of them.

"Do you suppose he'll find anything that might cause more trouble for the family?" Rissa asked anxiously as Drew drove away. "I've experienced all of the crises I want in the past few months."

"I don't suppose there's anything to find and Father won't talk. But it does worry me. Mick doesn't say much, but I know he isn't satisfied about the death of that P.I., Garrett McGraw. Although he's convinced that the police don't have all the facts, the case is closed."

They walked home in silence.

Rissa's impression of Drew Lancaster was that he would be a hard man to fool. Judging from the way his pleasant expression had stilled and become serious, he had obviously caught her warning signal to Portia. Would he interpret it as proof that the Blanchards had something to hide? Whatever the family had under wraps, Rissa figured that this detective wouldn't stop until he found out what it was.

TWO

Drew Lancaster's cruiser was parked near the gazebo, but he wasn't in sight when the twins approached Blanchard Manor from the woods. As they rounded the corner of the house, they saw the detective strolling along the driveway leading from the house to Bay View Road. He stared intently at the ground. Portia pulled Rissa into a secluded nook where they could watch Drew without being seen. He wore a dark brown leather jacket over his neat tan trousers. Tall and muscular, Drew carried himself with a commanding stance of self-confidence.

He had a camera slung over his shoulder and, as they watched, he stopped suddenly, lifted the camera and snapped several photos of that spot. He checked the screen of his digital camera, and, ostensibly satisfied, he moved on, with his eyes still watching the ground before him. Portia turned worried eyes on her twin when he stooped and picked up an item.

"I didn't check out the driveway this morning. What do you suppose he's found?" she whispered.

Rissa shook her head.

The sound of a car coming up the hill reached their ears and soon their father's Jaguar came into view. He was driving at his usual breakneck speed. He honked the horn angrily when he saw Drew. He swerved quickly and Drew jumped several feet to avoid being accidentally run down.

The twins exchanged troubled glances and reached the garage just as Ronald wheeled his Jaguar into his parking place and stepped out of the car, his eyes blazing with fury.

Although he was just a few years shy of turning sixty, Ronald was still as handsome and vigorous as he had been in his youth. Jerking a thumb toward Drew, he demanded, "What's he doing here?"

"Good to see you, too, Father," Rissa muttered sarcastically, but if Ronald heard, he ignored her.

"He said someone called about the commotion in the gazebo last night," Portia said.

His dark face irate, he lifted his arm as if he might strike her. Rissa choked back a terrified cry. Although Ronald had never displayed any love or tenderness toward any of his six daughters, she'd never known him to lay a hand on any of them.

"Did you call that boyfriend of yours?"

"No, I didn't," Portia gasped and stepped closer to Rissa.

"What did happen in the gazebo, Father?" Rissa asked, attempting to deflect his displeasure from Portia.

Ronald's eyes glowered down at his twin daughters, but he lowered his hand.

"None of your business," he said, before he brushed by them and entered the house.

He was detained when a firm hand grabbed his shoulder. Rissa couldn't imagine that Drew could have so quickly covered the distance from where her father had almost run him down to the front of the house. Ronald turned furious eyes on Drew, but he couldn't break the ironclad hold on his shoulder.

Drew's eyes were blazing with fury. When he spoke, his voice was quiet, but it held an undertone of cold contempt. "You're driving a little reckless this morning, aren't you?"

"It's my own property. I can drive as fast as I want to."

"Yes, you can, but you probably won't like it if I charge you with wanton endangerment."

"You wouldn't dare! I could have that badge of yours in a hurry if you make such a charge."

"I doubt that, Mr. Blanchard. You might not know it, but you don't have the influence in this community that you once had." He removed his hand. "I'm warning you—don't try to interfere with our investigation."

Without any apology to Portia and Rissa, Drew walked purposefully to his car and drove away. What could he say to them? Their father was probably a murderer, or at best, he had a lot of explaining to do.

Turning frightened eyes to her twin, Portia said, "Would he have hit me?"

"I don't know what to think," Rissa said, putting an arm around Portia, unable to reassure her sister when her own suspicions were rampant. "Let's go inside."

Through the rearview mirror, Drew saw Rissa and Portia follow their father into the house. Small footprints going from the gazebo and back again proved that whoever the woman in the gazebo had been, she had not been killed. He had followed steps from the gazebo to the spot where the woman had left her car. He'd snapped pictures of the tire tracks, but the rain last night had all but obliterated them. And it looked as if Ronald had swerved to drive across the tracks when he'd come home. Fortunately, Drew had already taken a picture of them. But what could he do with the clues he had found? He glanced at the key chain he'd picked up. There was no key on the chain attached to a porpoise in flight—a relatively common item found in gift shops. Could this key chain provide any new leads in the string of incidents that had involved the Blanchards for the past few months?

His partner, Mick, was in a quandary—trying to work on cases in Stoneley without causing trouble for Portia or her family. And now that he'd seen Rissa Blanchard again, Drew was in the same fix. Throughout the weeks since he had met her, he'd tried to convince himself that Rissa wasn't as fascinating as he'd thought at their first meeting. Now he wasn't so sure.

But he and Mick were cops first. Whatever their feelings toward the Blanchard twins, they were committed to upholding the law. He only hoped that they could do their job without bringing disaster upon Rissa and her sisters.

Drew rounded a curve and pulled to one side of the road. He locked the car and walked along a trail that took him toward the bluffs behind Blanchard Manor.

From this point he had a bird's-eye view of the house and the crystal-blue waters of the Atlantic. Rissa's heritage! He cringed when he considered how ridiculous it was for him to think about pursuing a relationship with her. She would probably laugh in his face if he asked her out.

And who could blame her? Rissa had been born with the proverbial silver spoon in her mouth. He, on the other hand, not only came from a poor family, but a dysfunctional one, as well. He lived from month to month on his salary, trying to help his mother support his two younger sisters. Financially he had nothing to offer any woman, and physically? To look at his strong body, no one would ever suspect the secret that prevented him from seriously dating any woman, let alone someone as special as Rissa.

The house was quiet when the twins returned and Rissa figured everyone was trying to rest after the commotion of the previous night. Portia went into the library to find Web sites for wedding consultants in Portland. Rissa went upstairs to the room she and Portia had always shared. Her memory was hazy about her life before they had moved to this house, which happened soon after their mother had died—or disappeared, as her father had recently revealed. She did have a hazy recollection of her mother rocking her to sleep a few times. Rissa was deeply immersed in her memories when Portia entered the room.

"I can't believe that our mother is still alive," Rissa

said. "Let's go over again what Father said about it. I was so shocked that I don't remember everything he said."

"He had faked our mother's death so we wouldn't have to know that she was suffering from postpartum depression. The best I can understand, she's been in a mental institution all of these years—when we thought she was dead—but she disappeared from there about eight months ago. No one seems to know where she is now."

"Could she have been the woman in the gazebo last night?"

"Surely he wouldn't tell our mother that he would kill her if she ever came to the house again!" Portia's brown eyes, so like Rissa's own, were full of pain.

"At this point, I'm willing to believe almost anything about our father." Rissa took off the boots she'd worn for their hike and stretched out on the canopied twin bed.

Almost immediately a knock sounded at the door. "Come in," Rissa invited.

Peg Henderson, Howard's private nurse, peered around the half-opened door.

"Welcome home, Rissa," she said, her sky-blue eyes brimming with friendliness. Peg had become a fixture in the Blanchard household since Ronald had hired her to take care of his father, who was suffering from Alzheimer's.

Sitting up, Rissa said, "Seems like I've spent more time here the past few months than I've been in the city. I'm going to wear my welcome out."

"I doubt that," Peg said with a bright smile.

"How's Grandfather?"

"He's having a good afternoon. He saw you out on the lawn and asked to see you, so this might be a good time to visit. His lucid periods don't come often or last very long."

Rissa hadn't been able to talk to her grandfather at all the last time she'd visited Stoneley, so she quickly slid off the bed and tucked her feet into her metallic leather slippers. "I'll come right now."

She chatted with Peg as they climbed the steps to her grandfather's rooms on the third floor, wondering how the nurse could remain so serene and sweet-natured when she had to deal with Howard's mood swings on a twenty-four-hour basis. Except for a few times when she temporarily left Howard in the care of Sonya Garcia, the longtime Blanchard housekeeper, Peg seemed content to stay with her patient. She did have a luxurious combination living-and-bedroom suite adjacent to Howard's, because the Blanchard family did all they could to make her life pleasant.

When they reached her grandfather's sitting room, Rissa summoned her nerve to go inside. In her most depressed moments, she had often wondered if she would someday be like her grandfather.

But Howard greeted her with a smile that was reminiscent of how she remembered him as a child. She rushed to his side and knelt beside him. If it hadn't been for him and Aunt Winnie, Rissa would have grown up without any affection. There was never any doubt that

Howard loved his granddaughters and that they were welcome in his home. If Winnie hadn't intervened with gentle discipline, Howard would have spoiled all of them.

"I love you, Grandfather," Rissa said hurriedly, for she wanted to take advantage of this lucid moment to let him know how much she appreciated what he had done for her. His trembling hand ruffled her long, curly black hair and moved slowly to her cheek.

"How's my big-city girl?"

"Busy, as usual," she answered. "The show is more popular than I'd ever hoped for. Tickets are sold out several months in advance, and I'm working on a new play."

"You've got the Blanchard drive, girl. You'll go a long way."

"But I feel very weak sometimes. I could sure use your help making decisions."

Peg cleared her throat, and when Rissa looked up, she shook her head. Perhaps Peg had sensed something she hadn't, because suddenly Howard's expression changed. Her grandfather was gone, and in his place was a senile old man whose eyes darted around the room. He stood up, and Peg was at his side immediately, encouraging him to sit down.

He clenched his teeth in anger and tried to push Peg aside, but she tenderly overpowered him and settled him in the chair again.

"Where's Ethel?" he shouted. He turned his tormented eyes toward Rissa. "Have you seen my wife?" he cried piteously.

Her heart breaking over the torment he must be

feeling, Rissa said softly, "No, Grandfather, I haven't seen her today."

"I want her," he cried. "Where's Ethel?"

His eyes, once so full of life and warmth, were devoid of any kind of expression.

In a soft voice, Peg said, "I think you'd better go now."

But Rissa wasn't ready to leave. She took her grandfather's cold, trembling hand and looked around the room, wondering what she could do to encourage him. On a nearby table she was surprised to see the Bible Howard had once carried to church. On the same table was a tray holding a large number of prescription bottles. Rissa remembered that her psychiatrist had told her that the Word of God could be a good supplement to her medication. Maybe it would work with her grandfather.

"I'd like to read to him from the Bible—maybe that will help calm him."

"It would be better if you'd leave now," the nurse insisted.

The nurse had the final authority on Howard's care, but Rissa begged, "Please, Peg, let me read a few verses to him."

Reluctantly Peg agreed. "All right, but sometimes he becomes quite violent after he's come to himself for a few minutes. I want to spare you that, but perhaps having you read to him will calm him."

Howard had had the reputation of being a cutthroat businessman and had been feared by many in the local community. Although he'd doted on his granddaughters, he'd been a hard man in dealing with others. But Aunt

Winnie had told the sisters that Howard had once been an active member of the church and had never missed Sunday worship.

His heart had seemed hardened against God as long as Rissa could remember, and she was concerned about her grandfather's eternal security. Considering his age and physical condition, he could die anytime. It worried Rissa that her beloved grandfather might go into Eternity unprepared to meet God.

She picked up the Bible, hardly knowing what to read, but she turned to the Psalms—a place where she often found comfort. But she must not choose anything to distress her grandfather. She glanced at Psalm Twenty-seven and decided that would be acceptable.

Rissa sensed Peg's displeasure and she prayed silently that what she was doing would penetrate that wall of spiritual indifference Howard had erected between himself and God. She had memorized favorite passages in this psalm as a part of her therapy, so she didn't have to keep her eyes on the printed page all of the time. Her grandfather didn't take his eyes off her face as she read, but his eyes were expressionless.

"'The Lord is my light and my salvation; whom shall I fear? The Lord is the strength of my life; of whom shall I be afraid? … One thing have I desired of the Lord, that will I seek after; that I may dwell in the house of the Lord all the days of my life, to behold the beauty of the Lord, and to enquire in His temple. For in the time of trouble He shall hide me in His pavilion: in the secret of His tabernacle shall He hide me; He shall set me upon a rock.'"

Rissa had no idea whether her words had penetrated the solid wall that blocked Howard's mind. She laid the Bible back on the table then leaned forward to kiss her grandfather's cheek. He lifted his hand and his feeble fingers caressed her cheek.

"Ethel," he murmured, and Rissa lifted startled eyes toward Peg, baffled by the amazement in the caregiver's eyes.

"Does he often mention my grandmother?" Rissa whispered as she moved away from Howard's chair.

"Once in a while he does." The nurse laid her hand on Rissa's shoulder and squeezed it gently. "It was good of you to read to your grandfather."

"Thank you for giving him such good care. Let me know when he feels like having me visit again."

"Yes, I will, but it doesn't happen very often."

Before she went to her own room, Rissa stopped before the large portrait of Ethel Blanchard hanging at the end of the second-floor hall. She had been a petite woman, as Rissa was. But her grandmother's hair had been red and her eyes hazel, unlike Rissa's dark eyes and hair. The twins looked like their father, something Rissa had often resented because Ronald had so little affection for them. But she was pleased that something had caused Howard to see a resemblance of his wife in her today.

At dinner, Rissa related her brief visit with her grandfather to Winnie, Portia and Miranda. Ronald had refused to dine with the rest of the family and ate his meal alone in his office.

When she mentioned that Howard had called her Ethel,

Winnie exclaimed, "I've always thought you favored my mother—not so much in looks but in disposition."

"Does that include me, too?" Portia asked.

"No, the few traits that you and Rissa *don't* share are the ways I could tell you apart when you were little." Winnie laughed slightly. "I'm sorry, Rissa, but some of them are negative qualities."

"Such as?"

"The way you frown too much, like you're doing now, or how you're often impatient. And you've always been easily distracted and more melancholy than your sisters."

Rissa closed her eyes, confused by this unexpected assessment from her aunt. Winnie should have added that Rissa didn't take criticism well, either, because her aunt's words had cut like a knife.

Perhaps Winnie feared she had upset Rissa, because she gave her a hug. "But don't let that bother you. It's the endearing qualities that I notice most. The tenderness and love you have for your sisters, especially Portia. Your determination to follow a project through to completion no matter how difficult it is. The gentle ripple of your laughter when you're truly happy."

"Enough, Aunt Winnie," Miranda cried. "You'll swell her head. She already has an overabundance of pride."

Rissa joined in the general laughter, determined not to be offended by Winnie's negative words. Obviously the family didn't know that her inner self was often at war with the calm, confident exterior she displayed to others. How long could she keep her depression diagnosis from her family?

* * *

After her long drive the previous night and the traumatic events that had greeted her, Rissa thought she would go to sleep as soon as she got in bed, but her mind was too active. Shivering from the cool breeze wafting into the room from the bay, Rissa got out of bed and closed the window. A flicker of lightning and a rumble of thunder alerted her to the approaching storm. She hurried back to bed and covered her head, aware that Portia was already asleep, breathing deeply.

Rissa had always been afraid during thunderstorms. When she was a child, she'd often run to Portia's bed when bad weather had hit. By sheer self-will she had stopped doing that when she was a teenager. But the fear remained. That was one of the reasons she had gladly changed the coast of Maine for the asphalt jungle of New York.

She seldom woke up when a storm raged around her apartment in the city, because most of the time she couldn't separate flashes of lightning from the street lights and neon signs. And the steady traffic along her street tended to cover the peals of thunder.

Rissa had discussed the fear of storms with her psychiatrist, telling her that it was storming the night her mother had died in a car accident. Because she had been only three at the time, Dr. Pearson doubted that she actually remembered the event. She suggested instead that, because Rissa had repeatedly heard about the bad weather the night her mother had died, she had learned to associate storms with thoughts of her mother.

Rissa delved into her memory for one of the verses

she had memorized as a talisman against fear. A message of assurance from the Thirty-fourth Psalm came to mind.

I sought the Lord, and He answered me and delivered me from all my fears.

Rissa repeated it over and over until her pulse ceased racing and her body stopped trembling. Strengthened by the Word of God, and knowing that such fear was inconsistent with her Christian faith, Rissa got out of bed, intending to face her phobia.

She walked to the window, pulled back the curtains, lifted the windowpane, determined to experience the full force of the storm. She heard the unleashed power of the waves splashing against the coast. Wind howled around the turrets of Blanchard Manor, and leafless limbs on the oak and maple trees snapped like gunshots. In the intermittent flashes of lightning she saw that the spruces on the lawn overlooking the ocean were bending low from the force of the wind.

A peal of thunder ricocheted across the roof of the house. A streak of lightning zigzagged across the sky, so bright that for an instant the room was illuminated as if it were daylight. Rissa stumbled backward from the window in terror and slammed it shut.

I sought the Lord, and He answered me and delivered me from all my fears.

Straightening her spine, Rissa stepped in front of the window and stared belligerently into the darkness. Seeing the humor of the situation, she laughed slightly.

"This is ridiculous. What am I trying to prove? Get

back in bed and go to sleep, silly," she ordered herself. That was easier said than done. It was futile to lie down when she was wide awake. Taking a flashlight from the nightstand, she looked around the room for something to read but she found nothing.

She sat in a chair near the window, and as the storm continued to rage around Blanchard Manor, she remembered people in the Bible who were afraid.

The psalm she'd been quoting tonight had been written by King David, perhaps one of the bravest men in Biblical history, yet he had often been afraid. *I sought the Lord, and He answered me and delivered me from all my fears* had been written when David had feigned insanity to escape from King Abimelech.

Jesus had often stilled the fears of His disciples, especially during tempests on the Sea of Galilee. Paul, the apostle, had known fear during many stormy incidents in his ministry, but he had never failed to trust God's power to deliver him from those fears.

The wind and thunder ceased and all was quiet in Blanchard Manor and in Rissa's heart, but in the distance she heard another storm approaching. Her thoughts drifted from the Bible to one of Shakespeare's dramas. Her favorite of the Bard's work was *Richard III*. A year ago in New York she'd had the privilege of seeing the drama presented onstage by a troupe of traveling English actors and actresses. Richard had been a wicked man and had feared no one. Determined to claim the English crown, he had ordered the deaths of several competitors.

At the end of the presentation, Richard had been unhorsed in the conflict near Bosworth Field when the armies of Richard and the Earl of Richmond had engaged in combat. Richard had staggered onstage, his armor clanking, fear evident in his trembling body, as well as in his voice. Terror-stricken, he'd shouted, "A horse! A horse! My kingdom for a horse!"

Thrilled as always when she thought of the play, Rissa had an overwhelming desire to read the saga again. Although she didn't know why, the family had always been interested in Shakespeare's works, and she was sure she could find a copy in the library. Carrying the flashlight, Rissa opened the bedroom door quietly. She descended the walnut staircase stealthily to keep from awakening the family. With her foot on the bottom step, she paused, feeling ill at ease.

One of the tall double doors into the library was ajar and she heard footsteps in the room. She turned off the flashlight, plunging the hallway into darkness. Considering the strange episode in the gazebo the night before, she decided it was wise to find out who else was awake before she went into the library. Rissa wasn't the only sister afraid of storms, so one of them may have come downstairs to read. She started to call out to see who was in the library, but she hesitated. Who would be reading in the dark?

A flash of lightning illuminated the hallway briefly and Rissa listened intently. Again she heard a sound— as though something was being pulled across the library floor. A tingle of panic rippled up and down her spine.

She instinctively turned and ascended three steps. But one of her sisters might be in trouble! In spite of her fear, she had to see what was going on.

A cold knot formed in Rissa's stomach. With her heart thumping madly and her body quaking with fear, she moved forward until she stood in front of the library doors. Her hand trembled as she pushed one of the doors wide open and peered around it into the room. She was momentarily blinded by a flash when a gunshot pierced the quietness of Blanchard Manor. Tiny pieces of wood fell on her head as the door she was hiding behind splintered by a bullet. Rissa choked back a frightened cry, knowing that she had to get away, but she stood frozen in the doorway. A thump sounded inside the room, followed by absolute silence.

Rissa held on to the heavy door to keep from falling. No one moved inside the room.

Was she dreaming? When she was on the first medication prescribed by Dr. Pearson, she'd experienced nightmares. But since she'd changed to a milder prescription, that problem had been eliminated. Rissa knew she wasn't dreaming now. But could her mind be playing tricks on her? She stuck her head around the door again just as a brilliant flash of lightning seared the heavens and made the library as light as day. A figure stood in the room facing away from Rissa, but when she gasped, the person, wearing a black mask, turned to face her, pointing a gun at her. Lightning flashed again, illuminating Rissa's face, and although she had no idea who was standing in the library, the shooter had surely had a good look at her.

The figure headed toward her and fear lent speed to Rissa's feet as she leaped across the hallway, dodged into the living room and slammed the door. Leaning against the door, gasping for breath, she heard footsteps fleeing toward the back entrance of the house.

Rissa knew she had witnessed a crime of some sort and she might be in grave danger. When she heard the back door close, she cracked the living-room door an inch and peered into the hallway. She listened to see if the gunshot had awakened the rest of the family. Apparently not. Except for the faint rumble of thunder fading into the distance, she heard nothing.

Should she go into the library and see what had happened? Had some member of her family been killed? She needed help, and she knew the only place to find it.

I sought the Lord, and He answered me and delivered me from all my fears.

God, what should I do?

THREE

In spite of her terror, Rissa realized that someone might be lying injured or dead in the library. Some member of her family may be bleeding, needing help, because who else would have been in the library at this time of night? The gate and the house were always locked at dusk and no one could enter by the driveway without the security code or by being admitted by someone in the house.

Perhaps she should summon help, but to prove she had overcome her fear, Rissa was determined to straighten out the situation alone. Squaring her shoulders, she headed toward the library door. On the library threshold her determination faltered. Fear gnawed away at her confidence.

She listened intently, but she heard nothing inside the room. No movement. No breathing. Nothing, except the ticking of the mantel clock.

He answered me and delivered me from all my fears.

No matter how many Scripture verses she repeated, Rissa knew she would never generate enough courage to go in the library alone. Who should she wake to go with her?

Miranda was the most likely one to ask for help, because her oldest sister could always handle any crisis inside the house. Her mind fluttering with anxiety, and clutching the banister for support, Rissa ran upstairs as fast as she could, her bare feet slapping on the cold stair treads. Pausing before Miranda's door, she lifted her right hand and knocked.

"Who is it?" Miranda's voice came from the other side, proving that *she* wasn't lying on the library floor.

Turning the knob on the door, Rissa said, "It's me—Rissa."

"What's wrong?"

"Something has happened in the library."

"What?"

"I think somebody has been shot."

Miranda tossed the covers to one side and grabbed a robe from the foot of the bed. "I thought I heard a shot," she said anxiously, "but the storm was so violent about that time, I decided I'd been mistaken." She rushed toward the door. "Who's been shot?"

"I don't know. Somebody was pointing a gun at me, and I was afraid to go in alone." As they hurried downstairs, in a half whisper Rissa explained why she had gone to the library and what she had heard.

Miranda paused. "The shooter may be still in the library. We'd better call Father."

"I don't think anyone is there now. I heard someone leaving by the back door, and it was quiet in the library after that."

With Miranda beside her, Rissa felt her courage returning, and she stepped to the door of the library and felt along the right wall for the light switch. Her hand hovered over the switch briefly. Her fears surfaced again. Did she *want* to know what had happened in the library? If there had been a murder, the shooter had gotten a clear view of her face. Because she was a witness, would she be the next victim? Reaching into the depth of her spiritual reservoir, Rissa took a deep breath for courage and flipped the switch.

Rissa and Miranda entered the library together. They stared wordlessly at the body of a woman—a stranger—lying on her back beside the fireplace with blood oozing from a hole in her chest and spreading over the black jacket she wore. Clinging to one another, the two sisters moved into the room. Miranda knelt on the floor and checked the woman's wrist and throat for a pulse.

"She's dead."

Rissa had never been this close to anyone who had recently died, and to her, the woman seemed to be asleep, although an agonized expression was on her face.

"How could a stranger have gotten into this house tonight?"

Miranda spoke in a tortured whisper. "I'm not sure she's a stranger." Her golden-brown eyes held a faraway look in them as she stared upward at Rissa.

Stunned by Miranda's words, Rissa took a sharp breath and stared wordlessly. Miranda laid her hand on the woman's cheek and sifted a few strands of the soft hair through her fingers.

"She looks like Mama," Miranda said.

Rissa took a closer look at this woman who might be her mother. A few weeks ago their sister Bianca had been given a picture by her now-boyfriend, Leo Santiago, of Trudy Blanchard and Leo's mom, a friend of hers. Rissa had been amazed at how much her youngest sister, Juliet, resembled the woman in the picture. And this woman on the floor *did* look remarkably like Juliet.

"Shouldn't we call the police?"

"I'll do that while you go upstairs and get Father, Aunt Winnie and Portia. They should be told before the cops get here."

Rissa took the steps two at a time. She woke Winnie and Portia first. She walked rapidly down a short hallway to the left at the top of the staircase and knocked on her father's door. No response. She knocked several times and then dared to open the door. What if he was also dead? She turned on a light. But Ronald wasn't in his bed.

Had her father been the masked man behind the gun? She dismissed the thought as silly—why be masked in his own house?—as she hurried downstairs and entered the library right behind Winnie and Portia.

Winnie stared at the corpse and she murmured, "It could be Trudy. Even allowing for the changes the years would have made, I think it's her."

Rissa put her arm around Portia and held her tight. Portia's dark eyes were lackluster with disbelief.

"Ronald will know," Winnie said. She looked toward the hall and the staircase. "Did you wake him?"

Rissa lifted her hand to her lips and she began to

shake as dreadful pictures built in her mind. "He wasn't in his room—his bed hadn't been slept in."

"Oh, no!" Winnie said. "Don't even think it. Ronald wouldn't do this!"

"Ronald wouldn't do what?"

The four women pivoted almost as one toward Ronald, who stood in the doorway. Standing close together they completely hid the body.

"Where have you been?" Winnie asked. "Rissa said you weren't in your room."

"I was reading in my office. I came out when I heard steps running down the hall and Winnie speaking."

The sound of sirens approaching the house caused rivulets of fear to cascade along Rissa's spine.

"What's wrong?" Ronald demanded. "What are you hiding? Step aside."

Winnie looked at the three sisters and nodded. The shock of discovery hit Ronald full force when his family obeyed his command. His mouth dropped open, and he stared, complete surprise on his face. Any suspicion that her father had killed this woman fled Rissa's mind immediately. Her father wasn't a good enough actor to have feigned this shock. But would the police believe it?

Ronald dropped on his knees and in a voice barely above a whisper, he cried, "Oh, Trudy, Trudy, have I lost you again?" He took an emerald-green silk scarf from the woman's neck and lifted it to his lips.

"We were in Milan on our honeymoon when I bought you this scarf because the color matched your eyes," he said in a reverent tone that Rissa had never heard him use. "Have you kept it all of these years remembering, too?"

He cradled his wife's lifeless body in his arms, heedless of the fact that her blood was spreading over the front of his custom-made suit.

"I've never seen Father like this before," Rissa whispered to her sisters.

"Neither have I," Miranda agreed. "I remember when Mother died—well, left—so long ago. I thought he was glad to be rid of her, but he must have loved her."

The rise and fall of the siren came louder, then ceased suddenly as the police cruiser pulled to a halt in front of the manor. Portia rushed to the front door and struggled to open it. Mick Campbell entered first and Portia threw herself into his arms. Drew Lancaster stepped around them and quickly surveyed the scene.

"What's happened? Who is this woman?" he asked.

Sensing Drew's strength and compassion, Rissa hurried toward him, hands outstretched. "Oh, Drew, please help us. We think this is our mother."

Drew turned his eyes from the crime scene and grasped Rissa's hands. Portia was sobbing wildly in Mick's tight clasp as he whispered comfortingly to her. Drew wished he had the right to comfort Rissa in the same way, but he could do nothing except squeeze her fingers gently and release her.

"I am here to help you," he said softly. Even in the midst of this tragedy Drew experienced a sudden desire to always be at Rissa's side when she needed him—a lofty aspiration for a penniless cop.

FOUR

Detective Mick Campbell, a ruggedly handsome, brown-haired man, released Portia and stepped farther into the room.

"Ladies, you'll have to leave the room until we make our investigation," he said. No one moved and he stepped closer to the grieving Ronald.

"Mr. Blanchard, you and your family need to leave the room. We'll take care of things here."

"No! No!" Ronald shouted. "I want to be alone with my wife! Leave me."

Peg and the housekeeper, Sonya, crowded into the doorway, both dressed in their nightclothes, and Mick threw up his hands in exasperation.

"Don't anyone touch anything—this is a crime scene! Will someone tell me what happened?"

Rissa expected Miranda to speak up as she usually did, but a glance at her older sister convinced her that Miranda was totally devastated by the "second" death of their mother. Miranda had been ten when their mother had "died" and she would probably mourn this death more than any of the other Blanchard daughters.

Clearing her throat, Rissa said, "Miranda and I found the body—I'll tell you what I know."

"Very well," Mick said. "Wait for me in the hall, and I want the rest of you out of here so we can process the crime scene."

Her face pale with terror, Winnie said, "Let's go upstairs to my sitting room."

Reluctantly the women left the room, and Rissa, noting the determined expression on Mick's face, felt as the Christians must have felt when they'd been thrown to the lions. She didn't want to implicate anyone in the household, but she would have to tell the truth.

Mick took Ronald's arms and tried to help him up. "We'll take care of things here, Mr. Blanchard."

But Ronald clung to Trudy. Ronald, in his late fifties, was a tall, powerfully built man and Mick must have thought he needed help to evict him from the room. He took an iron grip on Ronald's left arm and motioned to Drew, who stepped to Ronald's side and grabbed his other arm. Ronald lashed out at them with his feet, without results, and the two detectives pulled him off of the body of his wife.

"I'll let you see her again before we take her away," Mick said as they steered Ronald toward the door, "but you must leave now."

Cursing violently, in a fit of anger Ronald jerked free of their restraint and bolted down the hallway to his office.

Drew walked with Rissa to the living room.

"Sit over here, Rissa," Drew said kindly, pointing to a leather couch. She sat down gratefully, because she wasn't sure how much longer her legs would hold her.

She felt momentary panic as Mick walked into the room. Perhaps understanding her fear, Drew sat on the couch beside her and took her hand.

"Don't be afraid," he said. "Just tell us what you saw and heard, then you can go to your family. As soon as the forensic team gets here, we'll dust the room for fingerprints and any other evidence. We may have to cordon the room off for a day or two depending on what we find."

In a composed voice, she explained that she couldn't sleep and had come downstairs to get something to read.

"I've always been afraid of storms," she said. "It's always scarier upstairs, so I decided to come down to get a book to read. I heard a sound in the library when I got to the foot of the stairs. I turned my flashlight that way and I saw that the door was ajar. I thought it was one of my sisters until I realized that whoever was in the room didn't have a light on. I went to investigate and when I pushed the door wider, somebody shot at me."

Tears blinded her eyes and choked her voice as she dropped her head into her hands. Rissa felt Drew's comforting hand on her shoulders.

"Do we have to continue this now, Mick? She's not able to talk any longer."

"I'm sorry, but we need to get your account while it's still fresh in your mind. For over three months now, we've had serious problems involving people at Blanchard Manor. We have to get to the bottom of this. The whole family may be in danger."

Rissa lifted her head and sniffed. "I'm sorry. I'll try to tell you what else I know, which isn't much."

Drew handed her several tissues from the box on a nearby table. She patted the tears from her eyes and blew her nose.

Rissa straightened her back and continued, "I still couldn't see anybody, until a bright flash of lightning lit up the room. The man was heading for the door, pointing the gun at me."

"Did you recognize who it was?" Mick said.

She shook her head. "He had on a mask."

"But did he see you?" Drew asked anxiously.

"Yes, I'm sure of it. My face was in full view. He…"

"Are you sure it was a man?" Mick interrupted.

Surprised at his question, Rissa answered, "Why, no, I don't know that. Whoever it was had on dark clothes and the mask hid the features, so it could have been a woman."

Her slender fingers tensed in her lap.

"Then what happened?" Mick asked.

"I ran across the hall and into the living room and locked myself in. When I heard footsteps running down the hall toward the back door, I went to get Miranda and we entered the library together."

Rissa was regaining her composure, and she considered how much more she should say. She didn't want to reveal anything that might throw suspicion on any member of her family. They'd had enough trouble.

"Was the gate locked tonight?" Drew asked.

"As far as I know. Miranda disarmed the security system and opened the gate when she called you so you could get in."

A car swung into the circular driveway, and Mick said, "That's the forensic team. That will be all for now. Go ahead and join your family. But you can't go back to New York until we get some answers to what happened here."

Eager to know how her two sisters and Aunt Winnie were handling the death of her mother, Rissa started upstairs to the sitting room on the second floor. But she felt momentary panic when she heard Mick say, "Drew, see if the back door is open or if there's been any forcible entry. If there's no sign of a break-in, we can confine our investigation to the residents of the house."

Was some member of her family responsible for her mother's death? She entered the sitting room where her sisters and Aunt Winnie talked in muted tones. Aunt Winnie and Portia sat on the love seat across from the fireplace, while Miranda paced the floor.

"I still say it was just an act," Miranda declared. "He's hated her for years for cheating on him and getting pregnant with Juliet by another man. Why would he be so sad over her death now? Knowing that Mama wasn't dead would throw a wrench in his plans to marry Alannah."

Rissa was totally surprised at this revelation, but she wasn't as shocked as she might have expected. The things she'd learned about her heritage the past few months had prepared her for anything. Speaking calmly, she reminded them, "She wasn't his wife. He divorced her years ago."

"Ronald never hated Trudy," Winnie said. "He may have hated what she did to him, because no one likes to be betrayed. But I agree that I'm skeptical about his overt grief. That just isn't like my brother."

Rissa looked around the small room and its two floral chairs facing a small fireplace where gas logs threw out a ray of heat. She remembered her childhood days when natural logs burned in the fireplace and she and Portia had played in the room while Aunt Winnie had done needlework. Suddenly she wished they could go back to those days when they'd felt safe, even if their family relationships hadn't been harmonious.

"What do you think, Rissa? Was he surprised?" Portia asked, startling her out of her reverie.

"I've never seen him carry on like that before, either, but I do think he was surprised to find her. I watched him closely when he came into the room, and he was caught off guard."

"Enough about Ronald," Winnie said. "What did they ask you?"

"Just to tell them what I saw and heard. The forensics people are here now—that's why they let me leave. Isn't it terrible to get our mother back and lose her at the same time? Are you sure it was her?"

"I didn't get a very close look before Ronald came in, but as far as I could tell, it was Trudy," Winnie responded, a faraway look in her eyes. "It's been years since I've seen her, and twenty years in a mental institution would change anyone. She was a beautiful woman, and I could still see traces of that beauty on her face."

Rissa suddenly realized that her legs were trembling and she dropped into a chair near her aunt. The silence in the room was broken only by the noise of the abating storm. She had always wished that she could remember her mother, and it was shattering to have finally seen her after she was dead.

She scanned the faces of her aunt and sisters, wondering what emotions they had experienced at the sudden return of their mother. The only positive point in tonight's tragedy was to know that their father hadn't killed his wife the night before in the gazebo. But since he had threatened to kill the woman he had met, it seemed to Rissa that the web of suspicion and intrigue had drawn more closely around her family.

The door at the end of the hallway was open when Drew investigated it, but he found no sign of forced entry. He called one of the forensics crew to dust the door for prints. With a high-beamed flashlight, he checked the hallway for anything the intruder might have dropped. He found nothing.

While the forensics team worked, Drew helped them by taking numerous pictures of the room and hallway. Mick made a pencil sketch of the area, focusing on arrangement of the furniture. It seemed as if nothing was out of place, so there must not have been much of a scuffle. Was it possible the woman had been killed elsewhere and later brought to the mansion to intimidate the Blanchards? But the coroner estimated that the body hadn't been dead more than two hours, which would have been about the time that Rissa had heard the shot.

Mick removed the deceased's scarf, which was spattered with blood, and put it in a plastic bag. They collected some strands of hair and the bullet from the splintered door, but when six women had entered the room after the woman had been killed, any one of them could have caught their hair on those splinters.

When the crime scene investigators and the coroner left, Drew went to Ronald's office and tapped on the door. "Mr. Blanchard, you can come to the library now."

Ronald swung open the door and brushed past Drew without a word. He paused on the threshold of the library, but he seemed to have his emotions under control. He stood beside his wife, and his expression grew hard and resentful as he looked down at her.

"We have to remove the body now," Mick said. "Which funeral home do you want us to call?"

"I'll take care of that," Ronald said.

"You can call whoever you want, but the body has to be taken for an autopsy before the mortician touches it. We're staying here until the body is taken away, *and* this room will have to be locked until we're sure the investigation is complete."

"There's no key for this door."

"We'll see that it's locked," Drew said. "We don't want anyone in here. That means family as well as outsiders. The door will have to be repaired anyway, so we'll put a lock on it tomorrow. Which mortuary do you want?"

Ronald swung toward Drew with his right hand uplifted, his nostrils flaring with rage, his eyes blazing. Drew stiffened and he steeled himself to resist the man's attack, but Ronald turned away and slowly lowered his hand.

He let out a long, audible breath. "Carson Brothers Mortuary," he muttered in a harsh, raw voice. Turning on his heel, he left the library, and Drew heard the office door close.

"Whew!" he said, with a tense look at Mick. "That was close! Now what?"

"One of us should stay here tonight to be sure no one comes into this room until we put a lock on the door. We may have missed some vital piece of evidence." Mick walked to the door and looked at the place where the forensics team had dug out a bullet. "We have to find the gun that matches the bullet we found. I hate to call anybody out at this time of night to guard the place."

"I'll stay," Drew said. "I'm uneasy about the family anyway. Something's wrong in this house, and I don't think any of them are safe. I've got a Thermos of coffee in my car, and I'll hole up here to protect the crime scene."

When they walked out into the hall, Rissa and Portia stood at the head of the stairs. Mick motioned to Portia and she hurried down the steps to him. Giving them a private moment, Drew walked upstairs and Rissa invited him into the sitting room where Winnie and Miranda waited.

"Mick and I don't want you to be alone," he said to

the women. "We need to watch the library until we can put a lock on the door. I'm going to stay in the house tonight, so you can go to bed now and get some rest."

"We'll prepare a room for you, Mr. Lancaster," Winnie said. "We have an empty guest room on this floor."

"Not tonight. I'll stay in the library, but if we decide that you need some continued protection, I may take you up on the offer."

Rissa walked down the stairs beside Drew. Portia kissed Mick goodbye and the twins went into the living room. Drew went to Mick, who waited beside the front door. In a low voice, he said, "I don't like to involve the family in this, but who else would have had a motive or opportunity to commit this murder?"

"We have to remember that the murdered woman has been gone for twenty-some years. She may have collected several enemies during that time and one of them might have followed her to the Blanchard property."

Realizing that Mick didn't want to implicate his fiancée's family, Drew said, "I'll spare you as much of this investigation as I can. I don't intend to do much sleeping tonight, so I'll try to get Mr. Blanchard's story." He patted the small recorder he carried in his pocket. "We don't have to make public anything that doesn't have any bearing on the case."

With a worried sigh, Mick said, "We're cops first and foremost, so I'll have to forget my emotional ties to this family. We've sworn to uphold the law no matter who's involved."

"At times like this, I sometimes wish I hadn't taken

that vow. The women of this family are too kind and gentle to have to deal with such a nightmare."

"I know what you mean, buddy! Watch your back," Mick warned as he let himself out of the house. Drew turned the lock and walked down the hallway to Ronald's office.

He knocked quietly several times, pausing for a short interval between each knock. Fearful images flashed through his mind. Had Ronald killed his wife and then taken his own life? Would Rissa be deprived of both father and mother in such a short time?

Feeling desperate, he knocked vigorously.

"Who is it?" Ronald shouted.

"Detective Drew Lancaster, Mr. Blanchard."

"Can't you leave a man to his grief? The door's not locked."

With a sense of relief and some apprehension, Drew turned the knob. Slouched in a leather chair, Ronald stared at him with belligerent eyes. "What do you want?"

Drew almost apologized for intruding, because the man did look wretched, but from what he'd heard of Ronald Blanchard, he had no respect for anyone he could intimidate. He paused when he was close enough to look Ronald squarely in the eyes.

"I want some answers about this murder. If you give the right answers, I won't intrude on your grief very long." His sarcastic tone hinted that he doubted if Ronald was truly grief-stricken.

"Anything to get rid of you and your kind! What do you want to know?"

"For starters, I'd like to know where you were when the murder was committed."

"I was in this room, sitting in this chair. It happens to be my favorite spot in the whole house."

"Why did it take you so long to get to the library? From what Rissa reported, it must have been at least ten minutes from the time someone shot at her before she and Miranda went into the library."

"I didn't hear a shot."

"Why not? Were you asleep?"

Ronald vaulted out of his chair but Drew held his ground.

"If you'd ever experienced a thunderstorm in this house, you'd understand why I didn't hear a shot. Blanchard Manor receives the full blast of a storm sweeping in from the Atlantic. For almost two hours we were barraged with this storm. The wind howled around the turrets, tree limbs smacked against the side of the house and thunder rolled like cannons across the roof. Sleep? Impossible! And as for hearing a gunshot, I couldn't have heard a full-fledged artillery battle taking place in the front yard."

For the next half hour, Drew threw question after question at Ronald without getting much information. After his first rage at having Drew disturb him, he settled down and his answers were terse, his face like a stone mask. He maintained that he had spent the evening reading, rather than going to bed, because he knew he wouldn't be able to sleep. He wasn't aware of what was going on in the library until during a lull in the storm he had heard someone running and his sister's voice in the hallway. He had entered the library and found the body of his wife, whom he hadn't seen for twenty-three years.

"Then let me ask you a few questions about the previous night," Drew said. "I understand that you and a woman had quite an argument in the gazebo. Are you sure you didn't see your wife then?"

"Don't you think I'd know if I met my wife? It wasn't my wife—I told you, I haven't seen her for years."

"Then who did you meet?"

"None of your business."

"But it may be some of my business, Mr. Blanchard. If you refuse to answer questions and don't cooperate with the authorities to solve this murder, you can be arrested and jailed for impeding a police investigation."

Ronald laughed, but there was no humor in the sound. "And just how long do you think you could keep me in jail in Stoneley? You still have a lot to learn about the influence of the Blanchards, Detective."

Determined not to be intimidated by the man, Drew asked, "Do you own a gun?"

"Again, that isn't any of your business. If you want to question me, you're going to do it when one of my lawyers is present. Get out of here and leave me alone."

Turning to leave the office, feeling defeated but hoping his feelings weren't apparent, Drew said, "Mick and I have decided that your family needs police protection. For tonight, I'll be staying here, protecting the house and preserving the crime scene."

"You're not welcome in my home."

"That's obvious, but you don't have any choice, Mr. Blanchard. A crime has been committed here. It's our duty to find out who committed that murder. If you didn't kill your wife, I'd think you would be eager to see the murderer caught and brought to justice instead of opposing our efforts. We also intend to place your family under police protection to insure their safety."

Drew turned on his heel and walked out of the room. Ronald slammed the door behind him.

Deciding he needed to become familiar with the layout of Blanchard Manor, Drew walked upstairs and surveyed the two hallways that branched off into a large number of rooms. He had heard that the mansion had fifteen rooms.

Winnie Blanchard met him at the top of the stairs. "Mr. Lancaster, let me show you to the room we've prepared for you." She turned toward the hallway to the left and he followed her. Pointing to the first door, she said, "That is Ronald's room, and yours will be across the hallway from his."

She opened the door into a spacious bedroom that was almost as big as his house. A massive four-poster bed with a quilted floral bedspread and matching pillows was placed along one wall opposite a white marble-faced fireplace with gas logs burning. An easy chair was placed beside a table with a reading lamp on it. Framed prints of Maine's seacoast hung around the walls.

"I turned on the gas logs to take the chill out of the room. You can adjust it to suit your needs."

"Thank you, ma'am, but I won't spend much time in

the room. I'm here only to watch out for your family. Tonight I'll be guarding the library. Starting tomorrow, I'll be patrolling the hallways at night."

"I sleep down this hallway, the next door on the left, and you can call me at any time. The girls' bedrooms are in the opposite hall."

They returned to the central hallway and Drew pointed to another stairway.

"The third floor is occupied also. My invalid father and his caregiver have rooms there. I'd appreciate it if you would avoid disturbing my father if at all possible. He has Alzheimer's and he's easily upset."

"I'll be as respectful of your situation as much as possible," he said, "but a crime has been committed and we'll have to investigate. That means checking out the entire house."

"I understand," she said, with unmistakable sorrow in her warm hazel eyes. Although Rissa's aunt must have been in her sixties, she was still slender and rosy-cheeked with a beautiful luster to her faded red hair.

"Do your servants live in?" he asked.

"We have a housekeeper, a chef, a chauffeur and two maids. They have rooms in the wing beyond the kitchen. One maid lives in Stoneley and commutes. Our gardener and other outside workers are only here during the daytime."

Drew didn't want to cause any further stress for the family tonight, so he called a patrolman to keep guard on the servants' quarters so none of them could escape if they had killed the woman. Determining to question them in the morning, he returned to the library and pulled a chair close to the door, so he could see the stairway and much of the central hall. It seemed logical that Ronald had met his estranged wife in the gazebo the night before and had gotten her to come back to the house tonight so that he could kill her. The murder might have gone off without a hitch if Rissa hadn't come downstairs and discovered what was going on. But if Ronald was telling the truth, and it hadn't been his wife in the gazebo, then whom had he met? Drew was convinced that Ronald had deliberately destroyed the tire marks left by the woman's car.

Briefly, Drew wondered if he was trying to fix the guilt on Ronald because he didn't want to acknowledge that Rissa was the most logical suspect. They had only her word that there had been another person in the library. She could have killed her mother and then fired the shot into the door during a peal of thunder. She had the opportunity, but what motive would she have had? Rissa had only been a toddler when her mother had disappeared.

Recalling his conversation with Winnie, Drew counted ten other people who had been inside Blanchard Manor tonight. He knew that most Alzheimer's patients were mobile, and if Howard Blanchard had left his room and killed his daughter-in-law, because of his condition, the whole family would be inclined to protect him.

Drew poured come coffee from his Thermos, and while he sipped on it, he replayed Rissa's story in his mind. Although she'd been nervous, he hadn't noted any sign of deceit in her testimony. He recapped the Thermos and stretched out his feet. His hands dropped to his sides and he flexed the fingers of his right hand. They slid down the side of the cushion, and he bolted upright. His fingers closed around two tablets of medication. He lifted them gingerly and inspected them. Had they been in the chair for months or could they have been dropped there tonight? Or had someone dropped them after the murder? Regardless, how had the forensics team missed them?

Angry at what he considered a serious oversight, Drew pulled an evidence bag out of his jacket pocket, dropped the pills inside and sealed it. He saw headlights beaming in the windows, and he hurried outside to the police cruiser Mick had sent to patrol the grounds. He hailed the car, and the driver pulled into the circular driveway and lowered the window.

"Take this to Mick at headquarters and tell him I found these at the scene. They need to be analyzed. I'll report to him tomorrow."

Drew inhaled a deep breath of the moist air and halted on the threshold before he returned to the mansion. He wasn't keen on spending all of this extra time in the Blanchard Manor. He felt like a fish out of water, and he was aware that a few days living in this house would only point out more vividly the wide gulf existing between him and Rissa Blanchard.

Generally, Drew was pleased with the profession he had chosen, but he had a feeling that solving this murder would create an irrevocable gulf between him and the

Blanchard family. He didn't want that, and he sensed that Rissa shared similar feelings. But how could he do his duty as a cop and still pursue his interest in Rissa?

FIVE

Rissa paced the living-room floor after Portia went upstairs. She didn't want to be alone, but she knew she couldn't sleep and she didn't want to keep Portia from resting. Her mind was still plagued by the events of the evening, unwilling to believe that any member of her family was a killer. She didn't suspect the servants, either, because most of them had been loyal employees for several years.

Because of the security system, it seemed unlikely that anyone could have reached Blanchard Manor tonight by car unless someone in the house had opened the gate for them. But it *was* possible for a boat to dock at a few places where the ocean bordered the estate. The fury of the storm would have prevented anyone from hearing a boat's motor, and a stranger could have walked up the steep hill to commit the murder. But a stranger couldn't have gained access to the house without setting off the alarm system. The more she considered the crime, the more confused she was. She had to admit that the Blanchard family had more than its share of idiosyncrasies, but she didn't believe they were capable of murder.

Worn out from pacing, Rissa dropped into a chair. Since she was the only witness to this murder, she couldn't return to New York anytime soon. And it might put the kibosh on her shopping trip with Portia. Rissa could see her play career going down the drain while she was stuck in Stoneley. It would be impossible for her to concentrate on writing in this tense atmosphere.

Because the night had been so distressing, it had taken Rissa quite a while for it to sink in—her mother had been murdered. After believing most of her life that her mother was dead, she had only known a few weeks that her mother was still alive. Stunned by her own seeming lack of remorse, she wondered if it was normal that she didn't feel any sorrow over the loss of a mother she couldn't remember. The woman who had been killed in the library tonight was a stranger to her. It took more than biological ties to make that woman her mother. On the other hand, if it had been Aunt Winnie, she would have been grief stricken. Instead all she could think about was how her mother's death would affect her personal life.

In all of the stress of the storm and the murder, Rissa had forgotten to take her medication. If she went upstairs now, she would disturb Portia, but she had to control her tension. Reading usually settled her nerves. The library was off-limits, so she couldn't read *Richard III* as she had wanted to do. She checked the small bookcase in the family room, but it didn't offer much that interested her. She finally chose a commentary on fifteenth-century England. That should be dull enough to put her to sleep without any pills.

She carried it to one of the settees and stuffed a few pillows behind her back to lounge comfortably. She turned on the floor lamp for enough light to read. But the book was more interesting than she had anticipated, and as she read of the castles and manor houses, she could see possibilities of including these facts in a play. She admired the architecture of the buildings that were illustrated, but she shuddered when she read about the dungeons and means of torture during that era.

A scream sounded through the room and Rissa sat up in alarm. The book she'd been reading was lying on the floor, and Rissa rubbed her eyes, realizing that she'd been asleep. Had she heard a scream or had she been dreaming? She sat up and listened. She knew she hadn't been dreaming when she heard a woman's faint yet plaintive wail. Was Aunt Winnie or one of her sisters in trouble? She stood up quickly to go help the woman, but her pulse was racing and cold sweat covered her trembling body.

The symptoms were similar to the kind she had repeatedly experienced before she'd gone to Dr. Pearson. Had she heard a woman scream or was it a dream? She dropped back on the couch, her head in her hands. Was she losing her mind? She remembered what Dr. Pearson had mentioned about leaning on her faith when these attacks came. She tried hard to remember a verse of Scripture that would ease her mental turmoil, but her mind was blank.

* * *

Drew had just returned to the library after he'd checked all the doors in the house and settled into a chair when Rissa's scream brought him to his feet. He'd noticed that she hadn't gone upstairs when Portia had, but he thought she might have headed up while he was busy checking the rest of the house. A light was still on in the living room and he headed in that direction.

He looked in the half-open door before Rissa knew he was there. His heart went out her when he saw her trembling body and how she was rocking back and forth in agony. Feeling as though he was spying on her, he knocked softly.

Rissa lifted her head like a startled fawn.

"Are you all right?"

She shook her head.

"Can I come in?"

She closed her eyes and nodded. He knelt on the floor beside her.

In a piteous voice, she whispered, "Did you hear a woman crying?"

"I heard someone scream here in the library. I thought it was you."

"Oh, no, it wasn't me," she protested. "It sounded like it came from far away. Please say it wasn't me."

Alarmed by her distress and the wild look in her eyes, he said quickly, "I heard a scream, but I'm not sure where it came from. Maybe you cried out in your sleep. You've had enough stress tonight to cause nightmares." Somehow Drew sensed that he wasn't getting through to her, but he continued, "I'm sorry about your mother's death. It must have been a terrible shock to find her body."

"Yes, it was," she said piteously.

Shaking her head back and forth, tears slid over her pale cheeks. Without considering the propriety of his actions, Drew sat beside her on the settee and pulled her into a soft, impersonal embrace. He half expected her to pull away, but after a few minutes, Rissa became quiet, and he thought she might have fallen asleep.

Rissa had never felt so secure. Still, she wondered if it was wise for her to let Drew comfort her. But after the emotional stress she'd been under all evening, Rissa allowed herself the luxury of feeling protected. Forgetting the woman's cry for a moment, Rissa now had a better understanding of why Portia was so eager to marry Mick. She had never doubted before that her career was all she needed in life, but now she wondered if she was missing something vitally important.

Rissa hadn't envied her twin's happiness because she wanted what marriage would bring. Portia loved children and was eagerly looking forward to becoming Kaitlyn's stepmother. But Portia would make a good wife and mother. Rissa wouldn't. Her twin had apparently gotten all of the maternal instincts that should have been divided between them. She couldn't imagine herself as a mother, and she thought most men wanted children, especially a son. Would anyone want to marry her unless she was willing to start a family?

Hoping to calm her, Drew tried to think of something to talk about that would take her mind off the nightmare.

"Nerissa," he said contemplatively. "I don't believe I've known anyone else who had the name."

The uneasiness left her eyes to be replaced by a nostalgic expression. "Unless you're a student of Shakespeare, I don't suppose you would have heard the name."

"You've lost me there, ma'am. I've heard of Shakespeare, but I've never read any of his stuff."

Rissa sighed. "My sisters and I learned about Shakespeare before we studied our ABC's, I think. All of us were named for characters in his works. We have most of his works on our library shelves."

Drew's reading was pretty much limited to *National Geographic* and the local newspaper. All he knew about Shakespeare was that he had lived in England hundreds of years ago. He couldn't imagine why anyone would be so wrapped up in ancient literature that they would name their children after the characters.

"I don't know why, but my mother was a Shakespeare enthusiast. I won't bore you with all the details. Miranda's name came from *The Tempest*. Bianca was named after a character in *The Taming of the Shrew*. Cordelia's name was taken from *King Lear,* although we've always called her Delia. Portia and Nerissa were characters in *The Merchant of Venice*. And of course you've heard of *Romeo and Juliet*—that's where our baby sister, Juliet, got her name."

Drew shook his head in disbelief and stared at her intently. "I remember being introduced to Shakespeare in English literature during my high school years, but I haven't given him a thought since." He shrugged dismissively. "It's unbelievable to me that anybody in today's world would still be interested."

"If you ever come to the city, I'd like to take you to see a production of one of Shakespeare's plays. There's always a great production in Central Park every summer. You'd really enjoy it."

Noting his skeptical expression, Rissa knew she hadn't convinced him.

"Are you ready to go upstairs to bed?" Drew asked softly. "It's still a few hours until daylight."

Sighing, she moved away from the comfort of his arms. "I'll stay here the rest of the night," she said. "If I go to our room, I'd wake Portia. I'll try to sleep, but the nightmare is still vivid in my mind. I swear I heard a woman crying. I haven't been sleeping well the past few months, but I've never had this happen before. Thanks for helping, Drew."

He stood awkwardly, knowing that he had been excused, but from the tension on her face, he wasn't sure she should stay alone.

"I'll be across the hall if you need me, but try to get some sleep. Nothing's going to happen with me on guard. I'll see you in the morning."

He stopped in the hallway and picked up a small bell from a collection of odds and ends in the massive walnut secretary beneath the stairway. He closed the library door and hung the bell over one of the knobs so he would know if anyone tried to enter the room. He walked throughout the first floor, checking all of the rooms, even the hallway where the staff members were housed. He heard nothing, but the tour had provided him with more evidence of the wealth of the Blanchards.

He returned to the library, removed the bell and sat in the chair to watch. He remembered the feel of Rissa's slender body in his arms. How happy he'd been to know that she had trusted him that much. When he had first met Rissa several weeks ago, he had thought she was snobbish and pretentious, but in the past few hours, he'd seen another side to her.

He was conscious that she seemed to harbor an insecurity similar to his own, but he was puzzled why any woman who had everything going for her, as Rissa Blanchard seemed to have, would be insecure. He considered her a very special person. At their first meeting, he'd sensed an emotional current between them, which he hadn't forgotten even after Rissa had returned to her life in Manhattan.

During the past few hours, he'd been even more aware of the budding physical attraction between them, and he believed that Rissa was also conscious of it. But it would take more than chemistry for a relationship to develop between them. Recalling their discussion about Shakespeare, he was vividly aware of the great differences. Drew scoffed at himself for entertaining any romantic ideas about her. He had nothing to offer a woman and the sooner he accepted that fact, the better off he would be.

At daylight, Mick sent another patrolman to stand watch, and Drew headed home. Accepting his role of watchdog for the Blanchard family, he would need to pack a bag before he returned. He would also need to see that his parrot, Rudolph, had enough food and water to last for a couple of days.

After a shower, Drew tumbled into bed. He wasn't thrilled about staying in the house round-the-clock. On his first meeting with Rissa, he'd decided that she was stuck-up and considered him below her touch. But the way she had run to him asking for his help as he'd entered the house… He wondered if he hadn't misjudged her. When he had grasped her hands, he had experienced a sense of awareness of her that had nothing to do with his need to comfort her. He would see Rissa often if he stayed in the house, and he feared he might become more interested in her than he should. All of his life he'd heard that, like water and oil, rich and poor didn't mix. He was poor. Rissa was rich. He would have to be on his guard constantly to be sure that, when he parted from the Blanchards at the end of this investigation, he didn't leave his heart with Rissa.

Rissa heard Drew when he left the house, and while his relief guard was inside the library, she slipped upstairs. She wanted to shower and dress before the rest of the household woke.

She smelled food, which indicated that Andre was preparing breakfast as if nothing had happened in the house the night before. Surely someone had notified the chef about the murder, but during the stress of finding Trudy's body, no one may have remembered to tell the servants. Their quarters were not close to the library, and they probably slept through the whole episode. If so, someone else would have to notify them.

By the time she had showered and dressed in a pair of black palazzo pants and a silk blouse, Rissa heard sounds of the household awakening. Overhead, Peg's deliberate steps crisscrossed the small kitchen where she prepared breakfast for Howard.

Listening at her aunt's door for a moment, she heard Winnie's footsteps and she knocked. Winnie opened the door cautiously, and Rissa guessed that she was alert for more trouble.

Rissa stepped inside the room, where the bed was already made. In spite of the maid service, Winnie usually made her own bed, but perhaps, like herself, her aunt had not gone to bed at all.

"Did you get any rest?" she asked, wondering if Winnie had heard the woman's wailing call. She wouldn't ask, because she didn't want her family to know about her emotional distress.

"Very little. And you?"

"I spent the night on one of the settees in the living room. Now that I've showered and dressed, I feel much better. I smelled food when I came upstairs. Did anyone tell the servants what happened?"

"It didn't enter my mind, and I don't think anyone else thought of it, either. I'll go to the kitchen immediately. But regardless, we have to eat and carry on some semblance of order. If you'll check on your sisters, I'll tell the staff and meet you in the dining room at the usual time."

Miranda was already up when Rissa knocked, but Portia was still sleeping. Rissa touched her twin on the shoulder and shook her lightly. Usually Portia was not easily wakened, but she stirred right away.

"Sorry to bother you, sis, but Aunt Winnie said to tell you that it was time for breakfast."

"How can anyone eat?" Portia said as she sat up, yawning and swiping sleep from her eyes.

"Strange as it might seem, I do feel a little hungry. If you don't want to come down, Aunt Winnie will understand."

Portia threw back the covers. "No, I've been awake most of the night. I'll be downstairs as soon as I can, but don't wait for me."

Apparently the kitchen staff had been stunned by the news of the tragedy, because Portia arrived several minutes before the maid brought in the tray of juice and fresh fruit. The girl's hands trembled so much that Rissa jumped up and took the tray from her. Acting as if she expected a gunman to enter the room at any moment, the girl hurried out of the dining room like a scared rabbit.

"Many more episodes like we've had the past two nights and all of our servants will quit," Miranda muttered, as Rissa set a glass of apple juice by each plate.

Ronald's place at the head of the table was conspicuously empty. "Shall I leave a glass for him?" she asked Winnie, whose place as hostess was opposite her brother's seat.

"I suppose so. It's better to have it there if he does

show up, rather than listen to him complain if he doesn't have everything the rest of us do."

Winnie said grace and Rissa lifted her glass and drained it. She hadn't had anything to drink since dinner the night before and she was parched. And she was glad she was somewhat hungry, for she knew she needed strength for the ordeal ahead.

When the serving door opened between the kitchen and the dining room, Rissa was surprised to see the housekeeper, Sonya Garcia, rolling in the trolley. The short, heavyset woman was a fixture in the household, having served the Blanchard family as long as Rissa could remember, but there was a pecking order among the servants, and Sonya seldom lowered herself to waiting on tables.

The perpetual scowl on her face seemed even more pronounced this morning and her dark brown eyes snapped in anger. She pushed the trolley to the end of the table, leaned over Winnie and whispered.

"That's quite all right, Sonya, we can serve ourselves this morning." When Sonya returned to the kitchen, Winnie said, "The maid is so upset by last night's tragic event that she had to go back to bed."

Winnie stood and set the covered plates of food onto the sideboard.

"We have a choice of boiled or scrambled eggs," she said. She placed the tray of butter, jelly and a plate of toast in the middle of the table. "You can make up your own plates."

"I appreciate a little informality," Rissa said as they

filled their plates. "I'm used to taking care of myself. My breakfast is usually an egg sandwich and half a grapefruit. I eat it in the living room, in my office and sometimes in the bedroom."

Miranda sniffed. "You shouldn't get sloppy in your personal habits."

Rissa started to angrily snap that there was a world outside of Blanchard Manor, but remembering her sister's agoraphobia, she held her tongue. How frustrating it must be to fear going outside the walls of your own home!

"But Rissa is living alone now," Portia said, taking her twin's side as she always did. "It would be silly to go through all of this fuss for one person."

Ronald stalked into the room and sat in his accustomed place. "Excuse us for starting without you," Winnie said before Ronald could say anything, "but we were fifteen minutes late being served, and I thought you would have been here if you intended to eat."

Taking the plate of eggs and bacon that Winnie dished up for him, he said, "Meals are supposed to be served at the appointed time in this house, regardless of who is late. Winnie, I expect you to run this household as I run my business. Punctuality is vital."

Portia and Rissa exchanged glances, and Portia rubbed the back of her neck—their secret gesture that meant they were displeased with their father. He acted as though Blanchard Manor was his to command, while in fact, the property belonged to their grandfather, Howard. Because of that, Aunt Winnie had as much right to set household rules as their father. As she often had before, Rissa wondered why her father was such a domineering, cold-natured man. She thought about her youngest sister, Juliet, who had gone to work at Blanchard Fabrics, the family business. Rissa couldn't think of anything worse than to have their father for a boss.

Conversation ceased around the table until Ronald finished eating. Expecting a tongue-lashing, Rissa stood and said, "I'll clear the dishes from the table rather than ask Sonya to add this work to hers."

"Before you do that," Winnie said, "I'll fill a plate and take it to the officer in the library."

"Let him starve," Ronald said. "I want the police out of this house immediately. If we start feeding them, they'll never leave."

Ignoring him, Winnie placed eggs, bacon and toast on a plate. "I might remind you, Ronald, of the Blanchard hospitality. As long as I live here, we'll have no hungry people in this home."

She walked out of the dining room, and Portia broke the tense silence when she said, "I'll help clear the table."

Under Ronald's stony, silent gaze, the twins removed everything and put the dishes on the trolley.

"I'll bring the coffee and tea," Rissa said.

She pushed the trolley into the kitchen. The chef looked up and his mouth opened in surprise.

"Hi, Andre," Rissa said. "Thanks for a delicious breakfast. I'll take the coffee things in if they're ready."

He pointed to the tray beside the large range. "But I will do it, Miss Rissa."

She shook her head. She knew it was beneath Andre's

dignity to serve at the table, but it wasn't beneath hers. The silver serving set was heavier than Rissa expected, and she was thankful that the chef held the door open for her.

Portia had placed the cups before Aunt Winnie, who had returned by the time Rissa set the tray on a nearby table and placed the tea urn and the coffeepot by her aunt's plate. By now Winnie knew her family's individual preferences so she poured and Rissa carried the beverages around the table.

She encountered Miranda's shocked glance and almost laughed out loud. Had no member of the family ever waited on the table before? It felt good, very good, to serve her family.

Ronald drained his cup of coffee quickly and pushed back from the table.

"When you're all finished, come into my office. I want to tell you my plans for the funeral."

"Funeral!" Winnie said.

"Yes, you know—a memorial service to honor a deceased loved one," Ronald said sarcastically, obviously angry at his sister for defying his orders to feed the policeman.

"Under the circumstances, don't you think it's better to hold a private graveside service?"

"No, I don't. It's traditional for the Blanchard family to bury its members in style, and I intend for this funeral to be one of the most outstanding funerals Stoneley has ever seen."

His back ramrod straight, he turned and left the room.

Rissa was as stunned as her siblings and Aunt Winnie seemed to be. Why go through the farce of a funeral after Ronald had told his daughters their mother had died years ago?

SIX

Ronald stood in front of the fireplace when they entered his office. All of the office furnishings were crafted of walnut. The dark, massive furniture reflected Ronald's personality. He motioned for them to sit down.

"I don't know how long it will be before Trudy's body is released by the authorities, but I'm going to the funeral home this morning to make arrangements."

"Do you want us to go with you?"

His glance toward his sister indicated he thought her question was ludicrous. "I believe I'll be able to handle the situation without any help from you. I didn't invite you in here to ask for advice. I simply wanted to tell you that I'm expecting all of you to be here for the funeral."

He looked at Winnie. "You are to notify my other daughters of their mother's death and tell them to come home immediately."

He left the office and Rissa heard him going upstairs. She didn't want to stay in his office any longer, and she got up.

"Let's go in the family room," Winnie suggested.

Rissa didn't want to go in the room where she'd had the nightmare, and they couldn't go into the library.

"I'd rather go to your sitting room, if you don't mind. It's much more pleasant there."

"We should have notified the other girls before this," Winnie said, "but I'm still in shock. Trudy and I were friends, and I grieved when she died. I was overjoyed to learn a few weeks ago that she wasn't dead and I looked forward to renewing our friendship. And now she's really gone!" Winnie's eyes filled with tears.

"I'll call our sisters, if you aren't up to it," Rissa said, putting a hand on her aunt's shoulders.

Winnie shook her head. "No, it's my place to do it. I have their phone numbers in my sitting room. After I have my morning devotions and I compose myself, I'll contact them. I'll tell them of Trudy's death and Ronald's ultimatum, but I doubt there's any rush for them to get here."

As they were going toward the sitting room, Rissa saw Peg coming downstairs from the third floor.

"How is Grandfather this morning?" she asked.

"Quiet. He slept last night, but I have to go into town to pick up his medications and to run a few errands. The doctor doesn't want him to be alone. Would you mind sitting with him until I get back?"

"Of course not," Rissa agreed. "It will help me get my mind off of what happened last night. I'll come up right away. There's no need for you to hurry. Do you have a ride?"

"Yes. Andre is going into town. I'll go with him."

When Rissa entered her grandfather's room, Peg zipped up her coat.

"I just gave him his medication, and I think he'll be quiet all morning. He usually is after he takes it, but if he should get violent, ring for Sonya. You can't manage him alone. Promise me you'll call her?"

"Yes, I'll call her," Rissa assured her. She had only seen her grandfather once when he was overly agitated, and she didn't want to see it again. The time he had threatened Juliet at Aunt Winnie's party had terrified her.

Noting the blank expression in his eyes and the trembling chin, Rissa didn't think her grandfather would cause any trouble today. Tears threatened when she remembered how vibrant he used to be when she and Portia were small.

Choking back her tears, she waved goodbye to Peg. Rissa pulled a rocking chair close to her grandfather's chair and took his frail hand. The veins in his hands stood out vividly on the thin skin, as if the blood might burst through at any moment. Dark bruises showed on his forearms, and she wondered if this had happened during the times when Peg had to physically subdue him.

"I'm going to sit with you while Peg is in town, Grandfather," she said brightly, hoping for some response. There wasn't any.

Still concerned about her grandfather's spiritual condition, Rissa looked for his Bible, expecting to read to him. The Bible wasn't in sight, but she went to a bookcase and found a copy of the New Testament. She sat beside him again and started reading the Sermon on the Mount in the book of Matthew. She had no idea if she was doing this for her grandfather or for herself. She doubted that she could bear his wide-eyed stare in silence until the caregiver returned—she needed something to do.

The Scripture brought no response from her grandfather, but Rissa read on. When the clock chimed eleven, she realized that she had been reading for almost two hours. Peg would probably be back soon.

Still worried about her nightmare the previous night, Rissa decided to pretend that Howard was the same as he had been twenty years ago when he'd often protected Portia and her from punishment when they'd done something wrong. They had soon learned that if they could get to Howard and confess what they had done before their father found out, they were safe.

"Grandfather," she started, "I want to tell you about the nightmare I had last night. But the truth of the matter is, I'm not sure it *was* a nightmare...or if it really happened. It's not the first time I've had such an experience, either. So maybe I'd better tell you about that first."

She searched her memory to determine when she'd first started to question that something was wrong with her mind. It had been about six months ago when she'd been working long hours with the production team of her off-Broadway show. It would be her big moment— a time to prove she had made it at last.

"I've been having nightmares—or maybe they're figments of my imagination, thinking I see something that really isn't there. I've been seeing a psychiatrist, and she's diagnosed my trouble as clinical depression. I've been taking antidepressants for several months now, but you're the only one I've told about it."

Howard stared at her but she was sure he didn't understand a word she'd said. For a moment she agonized over whether her grandfather actually had Alzheimer's or if he was mentally unbalanced. After hearing that their mother had spent years in a mental institution, Rissa couldn't help wondering if emotional instability ran through the family. Most of her siblings had experienced emotional trauma at one time or another, and it was impossible to believe that her father's actions were rational. Anyone who would tell his daughters that their mother had been killed in an automobile accident when she'd left her children and husband behind because of her postpartum depression couldn't be in his right mind.

"Last night I fell asleep on the couch in the family room," she continued. Even if her grandfather didn't understand what she said, it helped to talk about what had happened to her. "Or at least I thought I was asleep, but I woke up when I heard a woman screaming. It was a terrible sound, a sort of wailing cry, as if someone was in danger or distress. But now I don't know what to make of it. Did I really hear someone or was it just my imagination?"

Rissa stopped abruptly when she heard a sound in the adjacent apartment. She looked expectantly at the door, thinking Peg had returned. When Peg didn't enter the room right away, Rissa felt uneasy. Was someone else in that room? She hoped no one had heard her confession to her grandfather. She walked quietly to the door and listened. When she heard nothing, she tapped gently.

"Peg?" When there wasn't an answer, she opened the door wide enough to peer inside the nurse's apartment, remembering as she did what had happened when she'd peeked into the library the night before. The room was empty and Rissa breathed easier. Perhaps a gust of wind had blown a tree limb against the windows. She didn't mind that Drew knew about her nightmare, but she didn't want anyone else to know. She closed the door and returned to the chair beside her grandfather.

"You remember my mother, don't you, Grandfather? Do you suppose I could be like her? I mean, do you think I might lose my mind just like she did after Juliet was born? But because it was postpartum depression, I wouldn't necessarily have the same problem, would I? What do you think? Can't you give me any help?"

Howard's expression hadn't changed once since she'd been in the room, and hot tears pushed against Rissa's eyelids. She got out of the chair and wandered around the room. She noticed the large number of prescription bottles on the tray on the chest of drawers. Could Howard be overmedicated? Maybe that was the reason he was so unresponsive today. Likely anyone with his violent nature might have to be restrained by medication. But she wouldn't question Peg's handling of her patient—she knew what she was doing. She'd been Howard's caretaker for years.

A half hour later when she heard Peg's light footsteps in the adjoining apartment, Rissa could have shouted for joy. If her grandfather had been his old self, it would have been a pleasure to sit with him. But her grandfather just wasn't here anymore.

God, have mercy on him. I'm no judge, but it seems that he'd be better off out of his misery. But remembering her grandfather's spiritual condition, she made one last petition. *I pray that You will give him another opportunity to save his immortal soul before he leaves this world. I don't think he's ever asked for forgiveness for his sins in years.*

Carrying several small bags, Peg entered the room. The wind that followed the aftermath of the storm had disheveled her short, curly hair and her fair cheeks were pinkish. Rissa regarded the caregiver in a new light. How could such a pretty, middle-aged woman be content to spend hour after hour with a patient in Howard's condition? It had to be dedication to her chosen profession.

"How did it go? I didn't expect to be gone so long," Peg apologized, her sky-blue eyes smiling.

"He hasn't moved since you left. Is he like this very often?"

"Most of the time," Peg confirmed.

"How much longer can he live this way?"

"It's difficult to say. I know it hurts you to see him like this, but he's strong. In spite of his mental state, he may live this way for a long time."

"That's a shame," Rissa said. "Let me know anytime you need me to sit with him."

Lowering her voice, Peg said, "Any news about what happened in the library last night?"

"We don't know anything yet. Father is planning a funeral and he wants the whole family to be here. He told Aunt Winnie to call my sisters."

"Some of the time when Mr. Blanchard is in his right mind, he rants and raves about his daughter-in-law, so I hope you didn't mention what happened last night."

"No, I didn't, but the way he is today I don't think it would have mattered."

"Thanks again," Peg said as Rissa left the room.

Because her grandfather was still mobile, Rissa suddenly had the horrible thought that he might have escaped Peg's supervision and killed her mother. It was no secret that he hated her, but Rissa didn't know the reason for his hatred.

Winnie had just finished talking to Juliet in Florida when Rissa entered the sitting room.

"Her conference doesn't end for two more days, and I told her to stay for it. I know Ronald won't have the funeral before that. By the way, I told the kitchen staff not to prepare a formal lunch. They're going to put bread, lunch meat, cheese and fruit on the sideboard. I don't suppose anyone has an appetite, but the food is there if any of us wants it."

"Is Delia coming home?"

"Because of the time difference I haven't tried to call her yet. I'll do that later on this evening."

"Has Father come back?"

"Yes, but I haven't talked to him. He'll make an appearance when he sees fit."

Rissa went into her room and stretched out on the bed hoping to sleep. She woke up two hours later feeling refreshed. Hearing hammering downstairs, she went into the bathroom and washed her face. She brushed her long black hair, dabbed on a bit of lip gloss and hurried to the first floor.

A workman she didn't recognize had attached a lock on the double doors into the library. Rissa's arrival coincided with Ronald's entrance in the front door, and when he saw the lock, he demanded, "Take that off right now."

Drew stepped out of the living room. "I gave the order to secure the room, and that's the only way to do it."

"I'll sue you for damages to that door, Lancaster!" Ronald shouted.

"The department will repair any damages caused by the lock, Mr. Blanchard. But the door with the bullet hole in it will have to be replaced, now that the bullet and part of the door have been removed as evidence. I assume that you won't want to keep it as a memento of what happened last night."

As he watched Ronald's back receding down the hallway, Drew was disgusted with himself. Why did this man irritate him? Probably because he was the number-one suspect in the murder of his wife, as far as Drew and Mick were concerned. But would they ever be able to prove it?

He turned around and saw Rissa watching him. "Hello. I didn't know you were standing there. I guess

I was too intent on giving your father a hard time. I'll have to apologize."

"I learned a long time ago that it never pays to apologize to him—it's a sign of weakness. If he thinks you're knuckling under to him, he'll make your life miserable."

"Well, you ought to know. Thanks for the tip."

"Is that your luggage?" she said, pointing to a small and a large bag by the door.

"Yes. It's been decided that I should stay here for a few days. We're not trying to be nuisances, but we are concerned about your safety. There have been too many crimes associated with the Blanchards in the past few months. It's frustrating that we can't get to the bottom of what's going on."

"I, for one, appreciate your help. You helped me get through a difficult night. Except for Father, we all feel that way. Stay as long as you want to."

"I'll take my things upstairs. Your aunt showed me where I could stay. I'll sleep during the day so I can keep watch at night."

Drew went into the room assigned to him, and as he unpacked his few things, he mulled over in his mind the strategy session he'd had with Mick before he'd left police headquarters this morning. He was sorry he couldn't be completely honest with Rissa about the reason he was staying at the manor. He *did* intend to protect Rissa and her family, but he would also be keeping his eyes and ears open to possible clues about the murder. In other words, he would be spying on the family, and he didn't like it, although he knew it was necessary.

Drew had been involved in other cases, and he'd only had occasional snippets of information about the Blanchard crimes. As they had considered possible suspects over their morning coffee, Mick had filled him in on what had been happening with the Blanchards. "Ronald is without doubt the most logical suspect."

"Because of his meeting with her in the gazebo?" Drew asked.

Mick shook his head. "Not necessarily. We don't know that woman was his wife. He had told his family that their mother was dead, but in the past few weeks, one of the daughters found out that she wasn't dead, but that she had been in a mental hospital for years."

Drew whistled in amazement, having an inkling of what made the Blanchards seem as dysfunctional as his own family.

"No wonder he's an angry man."

"He's also a devious man. Trudy suffered from post-partum depression, and Ronald convinced her that she was a danger to her children. She finally agreed to leave and get treatment for her depression, but she intended to return as soon as she was well."

Considering how difficult Rissa's life had been, Drew was glad he had been able to help her over the past several hours. "Then how did she show up here?"

"She escaped from the mental institution a few months ago, and information surfaced that Trudy wasn't dead at all. Bianca, a corporate lawyer, received a photograph from Leo Santiago dated *after* her mother's death and she started questioning the past. She hired Garrett McGraw."

"Oh," Drew said, beginning to see where this was leading. "And that's how McGraw got involved with the Blanchards. My gut tells me that's the *real* reason he was killed."

"Yeah, you're probably right. McGraw was a man who tried to play both ends against the middle. We're pretty sure he was trying to blackmail Ronald with the information he had sold to Bianca."

"Who else could have a motive and opportunity to kill Trudy?"

"Howard, her father-in-law. He's detested Trudy for years. His caregiver can't watch him all of the time, and he could have slipped downstairs, killed her, gone up the rear stairway and not been discovered."

"Is there a possibility a *woman* could have committed the crime? I keep thinking about those strands of hair we found on the shattered door."

"Sure—several of them. Winnie could have killed her unbalanced sister-in-law to protect the girls from her. And there's Alannah Stafford, who's trying desperately to get Ronald to marry her. She wouldn't have liked having Trudy as a rival. No doubt she's suspected that he's always loved his wife. And I assume she has the security code for the gate and the house, so she could go in and out at will."

"The fact that we don't have the murder weapon is only going to complicate the case," Drew said. "Let's send a couple of cops to search the Blanchard estate from one end to the other."

"And we can search the manor, but we'll have to get

a search warrant for that. I've heard from Portia that there are places in that house where she hasn't ever been."

"What about Barbara Sanchez, Ronald's executive assistant?" Drew asked. "I've heard it rumored that Barbara and Ronald are pretty close. There's been some insinuations that she's romantically interested in him. Does she seem like the violent type to you?"

"I haven't seen her often, but as far as I know she's levelheaded. She's apparently indispensable to Blanchard Fabrics, but I can't imagine why anyone who has to work with Ronald Blanchard day after day would want to marry him and live with him twenty-four hours a day. Someone needs to find out where she was on the night of the murder."

"Is there anyone you want to me to check out while I'm at the manor?" Drew asked.

"If you keep your eyes open there, that's all I expect you to do. We need about a dozen more men on this job, but we don't have the resources, so we'll do the best we can. I want to investigate Tate Connolly, too. He has no love for the Blanchards. Tate and Winnie were engaged as teenagers, but Howard tore them apart with lies and deceit. There was bad blood between the Blanchards and the Connollys for years. Tate and Winnie have seemingly patched up their differences, but Tate could have committed the crime to put Howard in a bad light."

"It's about the worst predicament we've been involved in for a long time."

Grimacing, Mick said, "And it's even worse for me than it is for you. I'm engaged to Portia, and it's hard to do my duty when my emotions are involved. I hate to do it, buddy, but that's why I'm shoving so much of this investigation on you. At least you can judge every clue for what it's worth, and not worry about having to arrest someone who is near and dear to the woman you love."

Drew stood and looked out the window of the bedroom. Mick's earlier statement seemed ironic to him. He was glad he could take some of the load from Mick's shoulders. And he could understand why Mick wouldn't want to arrest his fiancée's father. His own personal background prevented him from ever pursuing a closer relationship with Rissa, but regardless, it would sure be difficult to arrest Rissa's father or her aunt.

His mind refused to accept the possibility that Rissa had as much motive and more opportunity than any of the others to commit the crime.

SEVEN

Exhausted by the traumatic events of the previous night and day, Rissa and the other female members of the family soon went to their rooms. Rissa hoped for a restful night's sleep, but she was troubled about what had happened during dinner.

Aunt Winnie had asked Drew to eat with them, and Rissa felt sorry for him because he was obviously uncomfortable. He had no idea what to do with the numerous pieces of cutlery surrounding his plate. He had resisted Winnie's invitation, but at her insistence, he had sat down with them.

Ronald came to the table late, something he'd only recently started doing during the past few weeks when trouble seemed to be hovering over Blanchard Manor. He was halfway seated when he saw Drew. "What's he doing here?" he snarled at no one in particular.

Since there was only one other man at the table, there was no doubt about whom the "he" was.

"Detective Lancaster is here by my invitation," Aunt Winnie said, rising to her feet to confront her brother.

Offended, Drew threw the napkin he had just unfolded on the stack of plates before him. "I knew it was a mistake, Miss Blanchard. I appreciate your kindness, but don't ask me again. I *am* here on official duty and not as a guest. So please don't treat me like one."

He turned on his heel and left the room.

Rissa couldn't bear having Drew humiliated in this way, and she started to follow him, but Aunt Winnie put her hand on Rissa's shoulder and forced her to sit down.

"Ronald, how could you?"

"Why couldn't I?" he retorted, as he waited for the maid to pour his bowl of broccoli-cheese soup. "The man is out to ruin our family, and I don't want any of you talking to him. And I don't want him sleeping in the room across the hall from mine. Let him sleep on a blanket in the hall, as far as I'm concerned. He's supposed to be here guarding us, not sleeping."

"Do I have to remind you again that I have as much right to make decisions in this house as you do? It's been convenient for you to have me here taking care of your daughters, which has been the only joy I've ever had in my life. And now that they're grown, I'm sure you think you can drive me away. I won't go, and Detective Lancaster will stay in the room I've given him. After your tirade, I'm sure he won't accept any food, but he *will* have a place to sleep."

During the rest of the meal, no word was spoken at the table except to thank the maid who served their food. Rissa sent back her soup without tasting it, but she did eat a portion of the Swiss steak and a few vegetables. She wrapped two slices of bread and butter in a napkin to take to her room. She hadn't eaten lunch, and she knew she would be hungry before morning. She didn't relish the idea of roaming the hall tonight looking for food.

Once inside their room, Portia collapsed on her bed and started crying. Rissa, too angry for tears, sat beside her sister.

"To think our father would act like that," Portia said. "It's especially embarrassing because Mick and Drew are good friends. After that display, I'm sure I'll never get Mick to come here for dinner. What are we going to do?"

"I would suggest that you and Mick get married quickly. If he isn't welcome at Blanchard Manor, you can stay away, too. As for me, as soon as I possibly can I'm going back home. The way I feel now, if any of my family wants to see me, they can come to the city."

"I was surprised that Aunt Winnie invited Drew and that he even agreed to eat with us. I don't think Mick would have."

Rissa couldn't help but wonder if Aunt Winnie suspected her interest in Drew and had invited him for that reason. "She just wanted to be kind, but I wish she hadn't asked him. He was noticeably uneasy. I felt sorry for him."

Portia turned over on her back and dried her tears on a tissue Rissa handed her. "He and Mick have worked together four years or so, and Mick suspects that Drew has been scarred by the past, but he doesn't pry. Drew is a lonely man, not given to discussing personal matters." She yawned and stretched. Rissa moved toward her own bed in slow motion, wondering if she had enough energy to undress.

The sound of the knob turning on their bedroom door startled her. Portia rolled over and looked at Rissa with frightened eyes. Acutely aware of the danger lurking throughout the house, Rissa said sharply, "Who's there?"

"Miranda."

"Come in."

Miranda had changed to a long nightgown and a matching robe, but she was wide-eyed. "Could one of you stay in the room with me for a while? I just can't get the image of our mother lying dead in the library out of my mind. I feel so isolated from the rest of you."

"I'll go," Portia said at last. "I don't think I can go to sleep, either. I'll sit with you until you're asleep."

After her sisters left, Rissa roamed around the room. She didn't know how to deal with the circumstances of her mother's murder.

She kicked off her shoes and lay on the bed without removing her clothes. If she could summon the energy, she might take a shower before she put on a nightgown. The events of the past twenty-four hours had left her feeling unclean inside and out. Her mother's murder. Her father's hostile attitude. Her nightmare. Drew's humiliation. So much had happened that it seemed as if a month had passed.

Rissa gasped and sat up in alarm. That woman was wailing again! It was impossible to control her erratic pulse as she listened intently. Low and mournful, it came again, a plaintive moan that became a scream then faded into a whimper.

She didn't think she had been asleep, so it couldn't be a nightmare. She looked at the clock. Portia had gone to Miranda's room two hours ago and she was still dressed. Maybe she *had* been dreaming.

Once again, a terrible sobbing reached her ears, sobbing that could only have been the result of a flood of tears. When the sobbing ended and a howl of distress circled the room, Rissa jumped out of bed, and, suddenly energized with a surge of adrenaline that a few hours ago she wouldn't have believed possible, she yanked the door open, leaving it ajar, and ran to her aunt's room fearing her aunt was being hurt. Frantically she pounded on the door.

"Aunt Winnie! Are you all right?"

When there wasn't an immediate answer, she pounded again.

"Who is it?" Winnie said groggily.

"Rissa."

Winnie unlocked and opened the door. She was in pajamas, and her drowsy eyes and disheveled hair indicated that she'd been sound asleep.

"I'm sorry, Aunt Winnie, but I heard someone screaming, and I thought it might be you. I was so scared. Did you hear it?"

"I took a sleeping pill, and I went to bed right after dinner." The clock in the family room struck, and Winnie said, "It's only midnight."

"Did you hear the woman screaming?" Rissa insisted.

"No, I didn't. You must have been having a nightmare. Go back to bed. And lock your door."

Rissa didn't argue when Winnie returned to the room and locked the door behind her. She wandered disconsolately down the hall, but stopped suddenly when she heard light steps on the stairs. The downstairs was lit by the lamp on the table in the hall. Hand over her mouth, she waited to see who was coming.

"Rissa?" Drew's voice said quietly. She moved where he could see her. "I thought it was you. Is anything wrong?"

She moved down the steps to meet him. "Haven't you gone to bed?"

He shook his head.

One step above him, with her eyes on a level with his, she asked softly, "Did you hear it?"

"What do you mean?"

"The woman screaming again."

He shook his head slowly. "When did you hear it?"

"Just now."

"Were you asleep?"

"I didn't think so, but more time has passed than I thought. Aunt Winnie didn't hear the woman, either, but she'd taken a sleeping pill."

Panic was surging inside her, but she tried to shake off the building terror. "Miranda was feeling edgy and Portia went to her room to keep her company. She didn't come back. Maybe it was one of them screaming. Maybe something has happened to one of them."

She turned quickly and ran up the stairs. When she reached the hallway, Drew was at her side. A few hurried steps took them to Miranda's door. She paused, wondering whether she ought to knock.

She knocked quietly, and when there was no answer, she turned frightened eyes toward Drew. He opened the door and peered cautiously into the room. He quietly pushed the door back so Rissa could see inside. Miranda was lying in bed, and Portia sat in a rocking chair with her feet on an ottoman. Both of them were obviously asleep.

So upset she could hardly breathe, Rissa wandered back down the hall and stopped at her room, her face pale with worry. As they'd walked side by side, Drew had noticed that her body was as taut as a bowstring. He was concerned about her being alone.

"Come downstairs for a minute," he murmured.

She went with him without argument and he motioned her toward the living room. He took a pizza box off the hall table and followed her.

"How much have you eaten today?" he asked.

"Very little."

"That's what I figured." He commandeered a card table from the closet near the foyer and set it up in the living room. He unfolded two straight chairs and said, "Come and join me."

She hesitated. "I'm ashamed to eat your food after the way Father acted."

He dismissed her remark with a wave of his hand and held the chair for her to sit down. "Actually, he did me a favor. I figured I'd be like a fish out of water in the dining room with your family, and I was miserable. That's not my kind of living. You wouldn't understand my background any more than I can yours. You'd probably be miserable eating at my mother's table."

She didn't hesitate any longer, for the pizza smelled tempting, and she realized that she was hungry.

He opened the box and lifted a slice onto a paper plate.

"How did you get this?" Rissa asked.

"I'd already placed an order for the food before I came here today. The delivery came shortly before I heard you moving around upstairs. Your aunt gave me the security code so I can admit officers periodically to patrol the grounds."

"Did you go out on the porch to get the pizza?"

"Yes, but I didn't close the door," he replied.

"Then the woman might have screamed while you were outside and you wouldn't have heard her."

As attuned as his ears were to what was going on in the Blanchard mansion, he doubted that he would have missed a woman screaming, but he wanted to calm Rissa's agitation.

"Go ahead and eat your pizza. If she screams again I'll be sure to hear her."

He opened a bottle of soda for Rissa and took one himself.

"Tell me about your family," she said. "You mentioned your mother. Do you have any brothers or sisters?"

"Two younger sisters, but no brothers. They live near Portland, and I try to visit them once a month."

She hated to probe, but she wanted to know all she could about Drew. "No father?" she asked hesitantly.

An ironic smile twisted his lips. "Oh, I have a father all right, but I haven't seen him since I was fifteen." He decided he might as well make the situation as bad as it really was, so Rissa would know without a doubt that he had no place in her world. "He stayed drunk most of the time and beat up on Mom and me whenever he wasn't cheating on her. She finally got a divorce, and he skipped town so he wouldn't have to pay child support. I haven't seen him for more than twenty years, and I hope I never see him again."

"So we're more alike than you think," she said.

He snorted. "We have nothing in common. Forgive me for snapping at you, but I get angry whenever I think about my dad."

"I've learned that if I don't forgive my father for the way he is, then I'm the one who suffers," Rissa said. "Don't you think you've carried the grudge long enough?"

He looked at her, surprised that she was even interested. "You may be right at that."

"Do you read the Bible?"

"Not since I became a teenager and stopped going to Sunday school."

She pointed to a bookcase. "There are some Bibles on those shelves, so if you get lonely at night and want to read, perhaps you could read the Bible. I've learned a lot about forgiveness from the Scriptures. If you're going to stay up all night, reading might help you pass the time and give you a spiritual boost, too."

"I'll sleep in the daytime. I don't need a lot of sleep, anyway."

The pizza tray was empty and she found she did feel better.

"Thanks for sharing your food. You're good for me. When I'm with you, the tragedy hovering over our family doesn't seem so insurmountable. I think I can go to sleep now."

He held out his hand to help her stand and they moved into the hallway together. She glanced toward the library.

"Do you know when the autopsy will be finished?"

"Probably tomorrow or the next day."

"Father is planning an elaborate funeral and none of us approve of his plans—not that we have anything to say about it. He won't listen to us."

Drew wondered if Ronald thought he could cover his guilt by pretending to mourn his wife. He watched Rissa walk upstairs, pausing at the top to wave to him. In spite of his poor childhood, he decided he was better off with his family than she was with hers.

The house was quiet the next day after Ronald went to the office. A deputy stopped by with breakfast for Drew and after he ate, he went to the bedroom assigned to him to rest for a few hours. He wouldn't consider sleeping in the house if Ronald was around, so he decided to catch a few winks while the daily routine of the household was observed.

Although Rissa had slept a few hours after she'd left

Drew, she still felt listless the next morning. After a lunch of soup and sandwiches, she went to her room to rest. Portia had gone into town, and she'd insisted that Rissa should go with her. But her twin planned to have lunch with Mick, and Rissa wouldn't intrude on their short time together.

After the storms of the past few days—not only the rough weather, but the tumult roiling inside her—Rissa was happy to see the sun was shining. She had to escape, even for a short time, from the oppression of Blanchard Manor. She hadn't seen Drew since early morning, so she supposed he was sleeping. Not deceived by the bright sun into thinking the weather was mild, she went to her room, got a heavy coat and scarf from the closet and hurried down the rear steps and into the backyard. In a few months flowers would be blooming profusely in this area, but today, except for a few crocuses and forsythia, the lawn looked bleak and dull.

She started on the walk she and Portia had taken the day before, but a police cruiser was parked near the gate. An older man she'd seen a few times, one whose name she couldn't remember, stepped out of the car.

"Sorry, miss. No one is to be walking alone out of sight of the house."

"But I'm sick of staying inside."

"I can understand that, but you may not be safe. We're here to protect you—not make prisoners of you."

"I understand." She turned back toward the manor, which looked more like a prison than ever. She hoped the funeral would be soon, so she could go back to the city and her life there.

She walked from the gate to a spot on the lawn where they could see the Atlantic Ocean when the trees were bare. Several fishing boats were outward bound, and in the far distance on the horizon she saw a large boat, perhaps a cruise liner traveling between Nova Scotia and Boston. She sat for several minutes on a wooden bench and enjoyed the view. The cool air and exercise had refreshed her spirit, and when she entered the house much of her depression had eased.

She went to her room and removed her coat and scarf. The house was quiet and Rissa decided it would be a good time to take a nap. She had taken her medication earlier and she felt relaxed. She turned back the bedspread and sat on the side of the bed to remove her shoes. When she started to lie down, she saw a piece of paper under the pillow. Curious, she picked up the paper and suddenly the serenity she'd achieved during her walk disappeared like vapor from a steaming pot.

If you value your life, don't try to remember what you saw in the library.

The message was printed in bold, irregular, smudged letters, as poorly formed as if a child had written it.

Rissa threw the paper from her as though it were a hot potato. It fluttered to the floor and she kicked it aside as she rushed to Winnie's room. The room was empty. She bolted downstairs calling, "Aunt Winnie, where are you?"

Winnie stepped out of the storage room with Sonya Garcia right behind her. "What do you want?"

"I just found a threatening note on my bed! Come and see."

She turned and took the steps two at a time, but she had to halt at the top of the stairs to wait for Winnie, because her aunt paused to catch her breath midway up the steps. Her shouting must have wakened Drew, because he stood outside his bedroom, his hair tousled. Not waiting for Sonya, who was waddling up the stairs, Rissa rushed down the hall and into her room. Drew and Aunt Winnie were right behind her.

"The note was on the bed but I dropped it on the floor. There it is…."

The floor was as clear as it had been when the maid had finished cleaning it. No piece of paper was on the floor and the bedspread covered the pillows as neatly as it had when she'd entered the room after her walk.

Aunt Winnie's eyes were troubled and she smiled kindly, as if dealing with a fussy child. Exasperated, Rissa looked to Drew. Undoubtedly Aunt Winnie believed she was imagining the note. What did Drew think? For an instant, pity stole into his expression before he turned away.

"I tell you there was a note on my bed, and I dropped it on the floor before I left the room!" she screeched.

Winnie took her by the arm. "Come and sit down, dear. You're overwrought."

The torment in Rissa's eyes alarmed Drew, and he stepped to her side. Unconcerned about what Winnie thought, he put his arm around her. Judging from what Rissa had told him last night, she might be imagining things, but he had to pretend to believe her. Either someone was deliberately trying to terrorize her or she was on the verge on a nervous breakdown.

EIGHT

"What did the note say?"

"I can't remember for sure, but it was something like 'Don't try to remember what you saw in the library or you'll die.' You do believe me, don't you?" she asked beseechingly.

"Of course I believe you. Settle down now and tell me exactly what happened."

Rissa sat on the cedar chest at the foot of her bed and Winnie eased down in a rocking chair, as though her legs wouldn't hold her any longer. Drew glanced at the older woman before he focused on Rissa's problem. He picked up her hand, which was icy cold, and wound his fingers around it. "Tell me what you remember."

"I took a walk, then came upstairs to rest. The bed was already made, but I turned down the bedspread. When I started to lie down, I saw the note sticking out under the pillow. I read it, dropped it on the floor and went to find Aunt Winnie. She wasn't in her room, so I ran downstairs. She heard me screaming. We came back to my room, and it was like you see it now. The bedspread and pillow were back in place and the note was gone."

"How long were you out of the room?"

"Not more than five minutes."

"Did you see anyone in the hall or downstairs?"

"I was so upset, I really didn't look, but I think if there had been anyone I would have seen them."

"Only someone already in the house could have gotten in and out of your room in that short amount of time. Whoever put the note in your room could have been watching and had time to come back into the room and straighten up."

"But who would do that and why?" Winnie asked.

"It's hard to tell. But whoever killed Mrs. Blanchard may be trying to make Rissa believe she's seeing and hearing things that aren't there. If there was any doubt about her mental health, a clever lawyer might discredit her testimony should she remember something about the killer in the library."

Sonya had followed them and she stood in the doorway listening to their conversation. When Winnie looked toward her, she said, "Miss Blanchard, if I'm not needed I'll go on with the work we were doing."

"Please do," Winnie said. "I can't help you now." Sonya's thudding steps were soon heard in the hall.

Drew realized he was still holding Rissa's hand, and with a gentle squeeze he dropped it and stood up. "Who is in the house now besides the four of us?"

"Miranda and the household staff. Of course, my father and his caregiver are on the third floor. He seldom leaves his room and Peg always uses the back stairway instead of this one."

"We can't assume that someone couldn't have slipped in the house. Let's do some role playing. Miss Blanchard, you go downstairs and into the room where you were working. Rissa, you come into the room and repeat your actions. I'll time you to see how much time actually passed."

She reenacted everything, starting with entering the room, sitting on the bed and removing her shoes. She pulled the bedspread from under the pillows and folded it neatly to the bottom of the bed. She started to lie down, pretended to find and read a piece of paper.

Drew started timing when she dropped the note, screamed and rushed out of the door, shouting. He stayed by the doorway as she pounded on Winnie's door, opened it and peered inside. She turned and ran down the steps. She and Winnie returned together.

"Four minutes," he said.

"Could anyone move that fast?"

"They could have if they were in one of the rooms in this hall, or even in the bedroom closet."

"That's creepy!" Rissa said, shuddering. "Thinking I started to lie down when someone might have been hiding in the room."

"It's rather strange that Miranda hasn't heard what's going on," Winnie said. "Even if she was taking a nap, she's usually a light sleeper."

"Oh, no!" Rissa said. "Maybe terrorizing me was a ruse to get me out of the way so they could hurt Miranda."

She ran down the hallway and turned the knob on Miranda's door. It opened and she called, "Miranda! Where are you?" She darted into the room and shot out into the hallway again. "The room is empty. Miranda!"

The bathroom door behind her opened and Miranda stuck her head out. Her hair was wrapped in a terry-cloth towel and she wore a bathrobe. "I took a hot bath to relax, then I shampooed my hair in the shower. What's wrong?"

She saw Drew standing behind Winnie. "Oh, my!" she said, and her face turned beet-red. She pulled the door almost shut. "I didn't know we weren't alone! What do you want?"

"We'll tell you later," Rissa said, amused at Miranda's discomfort—it was the only thing she'd found amusing in the past several days. "We were checking to see if you were all right."

"She couldn't have heard anything since she was in the shower, so that accounts for that," Drew said as they moved back to Rissa's room. "I can't believe anyone in the house would have had time to act without someone seeing them leave the room."

"How long had you been out of your room when I came up the stairs with Aunt Winnie?"

"I saw your head as soon as I stepped out of the door. But I was watching you—if someone was in either end of the hallway, I wouldn't have seen them."

Winnie went toward her room, her steps lagging, her shoulders slumped in defeat.

Rissa said quietly, "She thinks I imagined the note

and everything. That's the reason she's so worried. You believe me, don't you?"

Drew hesitated only slightly. Remembering Rissa's nervous stress on a few occasions, he thought she might be imagining things, but he was convinced that she thought these events had actually happened, so he said, "Yes, I believe you, and I wish I could help you. If I knew the background of the people in this house, that might help me understand what's going on."

"I heard Father tell Aunt Winnie he wouldn't be home for dinner tonight." Her lip curled slightly. "I suppose he has a date with his girlfriend. I'll meet you in the living room right after dinner."

Because he sensed that her father's love life distressed Rissa, Drew didn't comment; however, it was well known in the area that Ronald Blanchard was a ladies' man. His latest interest, Alannah Stafford, was a rich divorcée. Alannah definitely looked upon Ronald as hers and she probably wouldn't take kindly to the reappearance of his wife, even if Ronald had divorced Trudy years ago.

"We'll talk then, but try to get some rest this afternoon."

She promised and went to her room. Although her body was weary, her mind was too busy to allow her to relax and sleep. She moved a chair close to the window and pulled the curtain so she could have a view of the bay. The sun highlighted the incoming waves as they dipped and swayed toward the shore.

Looking at her watch, Rissa realized it was time for her medication. She opened her purse, but couldn't find the bottle of pills. What could she have done with them? But considering her stressful homecoming, it was little wonder that she was absentminded. She went to her cosmetic case and a got a pill from the prescription bottle she'd filled just before she left New York.

She couldn't blame Aunt Winnie and the others, perhaps even Drew, for thinking that she was imagining everything that was happening. At times she wondered if her clinical depression could be causing the problem.

She rocked lazily, waiting for the medicine to take effect. When she'd been at her lowest ebb before she'd gone to the psychiatrist, God had led her to a verse in the New Testament, which had encouraged her when nothing else would.

For God hath not given us the spirit of fear; but of power, and of love and of a sound mind.

Admittedly in that particular verse, the Apostle Paul had written those words to the youthful Timothy to encourage him to be fearless when he presented the Gospel to those who did not believe. But Rissa had adopted the message as the antidote for her uneasiness. And she repeated the words aloud.

"'For God hath not given us the spirit of fear; but of power, and of love and of a sound mind.'"

Encouraged to believe that she did have a sound mind, Rissa stretched out on her bed on top of the bedspread. She wanted to be rested for her meeting with Drew tonight.

An angry, unseen figure moved silently through the hallways of Blanchard Manor. Another ruse had failed to produce the planned results. Someone needed to be arrested for the shooting before the authorities started widening their search. What else could be done to make them believe that Rissa Blanchard was mentally unsound?

Or was it necessary to take more violent measures? Perhaps another murder? After all, the elimination of *all* Blanchards could be considered a benevolent act. But which one should be next? Probably Rissa—after all, she was already on the verge of insanity. A satisfied smile crossed the features hidden from view by a hooded cloak. Yes, that was the answer. It would be fairly easy to arrange a pseudo suicide for her.

Rissa had always gotten along well with the chef, and after the table had been cleared and everyone else had gone to their rooms after dinner, Rissa entered the kitchen.

"Andre," she said, "would you let me have some extra servings of the chocolate-cherry torte we had for dinner tonight? It was delicious."

Beaming a smile in her direction, Andre not only placed generous servings of the torte on a silver tray, but with a flourish he also added some oatmeal-raisin cookies. Rissa threw the chef a kiss as she sneaked out of the kitchen with her bounty. Drew was finishing his meal from a fast-food restaurant when she approached the front hallway, and with bravado she lifted the dessert tray.

"Dessert, compliments of the chef," she said, wondering if he would accept anything from the table of Ronald Blanchard. "I didn't eat my dessert—thought I would wait and share it with you. We can eat in the living room when you're ready."

"You're too good to me," he said with an appreciative grin. "But I'm full now. Let's wait a while before we have the dessert."

"Suits me. My appetite isn't good, anyway. I have to force down practically everything I eat."

They moved into the living room. She took a seat on one of the settees and Drew sat on the other where he could face her. She placed the dessert tray on the table that separated the two couches. He spent most of his evenings patrolling the halls, but he wanted some information from Rissa, and it was best if they weren't overheard.

"Thanks for coming to talk to me," Drew said. "I don't expect you to betray anything about your family that you don't want to. But it seems as if Mick and I are stumbling around in the dark. No matter how diligent we are, crimes are still happening to you and your family."

"I'll give you as much family background as I know, but I feel like a traitor to do it."

"I can understand that to a certain extent, but if some member of your family killed Trudy Blanchard, how do you know that person won't kill someone else?"

"I don't *know* anything, but I'll tell you a few things that have happened and pray that it won't incriminate any of my loved ones."

"I agree to that. But to understand what's going on here, I have to know something about the people who were in the house this afternoon and why they might be trying to intimidate you. Give me a brief rundown on them—let's start with your aunt."

"Aunt Winnie has devoted her life to looking after us girls. She and my mother were friends and she kept the memory of our mother alive in our hearts. She's the most patient woman I've ever known, and she's a good Christian woman. I can't believe she would have done away with my mother."

Drew had pulled a notebook from his pocket and he made notes as she talked.

"I suppose we could discount your grandfather because of his age and infirmity."

"I love my grandfather and I don't like to think that he could have committed this crime, but he has Alzheimer's and he does some strange things. In January, when we were all home celebrating Aunt Winnie's sixtieth birthday, he came out among the guests and made a terrible scene. Our youngest sister, Juliet, tried to calm him down and he turned on her like a madman."

"So that means he can be violent. If he would turn on your sister during a dementia lapse, he could turn on the rest of you."

"I don't think so. He mistook Juliet for our mother because she looks more like Mother than any of us. For some reason, Grandfather always hated her. He called Juliet 'Trudy' and shouted that she had to be stopped before she destroyed the whole Blanchard family." Rissa shuddered, remembering. "It was terrible and so unlike Grandfather. I don't like to say it, but his hate was so intense that it's not out of the realm of possibility that if he was wandering around and saw our mother in the library, he might have killed her."

"But the night she was killed—wouldn't he have gone upstairs to his room? Your heard somebody, presumably the murderer, going out the back door?"

"I heard steps going toward the back, but there's a back stairway he could have used to go up to his apartment."

"Let's go back to his verbal attack on Juliet. What happened after that?"

"All of us were so shocked we didn't know what to do. But Peg Henderson, his caregiver, and Sonya, the housekeeper, subdued him and took him back to his room."

"All right, let's discuss them. They were both here this afternoon."

"Peg is a nurse who's been living at Blanchard Manor for five years—ever since Grandfather's Alzheimer's became so bad. She wouldn't have known my mother. She pretty much keeps to herself, but she moves around quickly, so she could have been in my room and back upstairs in four minutes.

"And as for Sonya, she's been here for years. Besides, she was with Aunt Winnie in the storage room checking the linens when I found the note."

"So that brings us to Miranda."

Wide-eyed, Rissa said, "Surely you don't suspect her!"

"I don't suspect anyone in particular, but I need some background information on everyone. We have to remember that everyone who was here today was also in the house when your mother was killed."

"Miranda has some peculiarities, but I can't imagine her ever killing anyone. She's always been bossy— taking her role as the oldest sister too seriously to suit Portia and me when we were teenagers. She stays in the house for weeks at a time, as if she's afraid to go outside. I've tried to get her to visit us in the city, and you'd think I'd suggested taking her to the moon."

"She must be quite a bit older than the rest of you."

"No, she's only seven years older than I am. She just looks older because of the dowdy clothes she wears. If she'd fix herself up, she'd look so much younger."

"But we can't rule out the fact that she did have more opportunity than anyone else to come to your room today."

"While I have bugged her over the years, I don't believe she would threaten me."

Drew checked through his notes. "Portia wasn't here this afternoon, but where was she when your mother was murdered?"

"She was in bed asleep when I came downstairs. She could always sleep through a storm. And when I rushed to our room after Miranda and I discovered the body, she was still sleeping."

Drew made a few notes and scanned his notebook. Shaking his head, he said, "This doesn't give me much to go on, but I appreciate your candor. What you've told me helps me understand the family situation much better."

Rissa fidgeted in her chair, her slender fingers tensed in her lap. Awkwardly, she cleared her throat. This wasn't going to be easy.

"Drew, you've been so kind to me in the past few

days, and I think I should level with you. I'm going to tell you something that none of my family knows. I've sensed that you've had some doubts about whether or not I've been imagining things, and it *is* possible."

His dark eyes widened in astonishment. She couldn't look at him as she told him, so she cast her eyes downward.

"I don't know if you're aware that I'm a playwright, and my first show is just now appearing onstage. I've been under a lot of pressure the past year. I haven't been able to sleep and sometimes when I do sleep, I have terrible nightmares. I reached the point when I thought I might be losing my mind. I feared it ran in the family, because my mother had postpartum depression after Juliet was born. I finally went to a psychiatrist, who diagnosed me with a case of mild clinical depression. She prescribed a low dose of antidepressants and as long as I take my medication, I don't have any trouble. But I can't explain what's been happening to me the past few days. It's terribly depressing to think you're losing your mind."

Her eyes came up to study his face and Drew was struck by the despair in her expression.

"You're the sanest person I know," he assured her in a calm voice. And he realized that he believed it—any doubts about her possible hallucinations dissipated like a heat wave after a gentle summer rain. "It often helps to talk your fears over with other people. Talk to me any time you want to."

An expression of confidence showed in her eyes. "There's no time like the present, if you have the time."

"I have all night long," he assured her with an infectious smile.

Her face broke into a smile, too, and she talked evenly as she recalled childhood incidents that had molded her life. "When I was a little girl, I was locked in a closet by mistake and no one found me for several hours. I was physically sick for days after that. A year ago, I was caught in a stalled elevator on the twenty-fourth floor of a high-rise with five other people. We were only in there about half an hour, but I was a basket case when we were rescued. They took me to the emergency room, and I was so hysterical they kept me in the hospital overnight."

Talking about her consternation noticeably distressed her, and Drew said, "Everyone has a phobia of some kind. My greatest fear is going blind. One of my friends in elementary school went hunting with his dad and was blinded when a stray bullet hit him in the head. I've feared blindness since that day."

For a moment Drew considered confiding in Rissa about his dysfunctional family that had marred his childhood. And also the medical issue that made his future look bleak. Maybe he would sometime, but not tonight.

"The psychiatrist also suggested that I take a daily dose of Scripture along with my prescribed medication and it has helped. My faith has become stronger."

"Winnie and your sisters that I've met all display a sweet humility, and I feel that this is a result of your spiritual life. After you went upstairs last night, I took your advice and looked for a Bible. I read several chapters and was surprised at how many of the stories that I'd learned in Sunday school came back to me. One teacher insisted that we memorize a Bible verse every week."

"Does one story in particular stand out for you?"

"The one that spoke to me more than any other was the parable of the Prodigal Son. As far as my Christian life is concerned, I've been wandering in a far country, and I think it's about time for me to come home. Mick is real active in the work at Unity Christian Church, and he invites me to go with him every week. When we clear up this newest case at Blanchard Manor, I'm going to surprise him and go with him."

She beamed a smile in his direction. "That will make me very happy." She stood up and started toward him. He met her halfway. She gave him both of her hands. "You're so kind to me."

He pulled her into a brief embrace, and Rissa relaxed and enjoyed the closeness of him. Being held in his arms made her feel secure and safe. It was the kind of caress she would have given to anyone who had rededicated his life to a closer walk with God. But she knew it signaled something more. She not only found security in Drew's arms, but peace, as well. Was she ready for what was developing between them? Without meeting his eyes, she eased out of his arms and moved toward the steps.

"Goodnight. You've helped me very much." She sensed that his eyes watched her until she reached the top of the stairs and moved out of sight to her room.

After breakfast the next morning, Rissa asked Portia to take a walk with her along the driveway. Even though she still felt like a prisoner, having to stay in sight of the officer who alternately patrolled the grounds or parked near the gate, she couldn't stay inside. Sometimes she envied Miranda and her mild agoraphobia, because she was content to stay inside the walls of the mansion. At times when her creative juices were flowing like a river, Rissa would stay in her apartment for a week at a time, living on cereal and crackers while she finished a scene in one of her plays. But for the most part, she walked every day.

Portia waited for her at the foot of the stairs. The temperature was much warmer today, and Rissa went upstairs to get a lighter jacket than the one she'd been wearing. But the wind was strong and she opened the top drawer of her dresser to get a scarf to tie around her head. As she rummaged for a scarf she often wore when she was home, her hand touched a sharp object. She lifted it and stifled a shriek.

It was a picture she had never seen before, in a gold frame. She had seen enough pictures of herself and Portia when they were little to know that the children were her twin and herself. Sitting between them was a young woman who looked like Juliet, so it must be their mother. Rissa had taken a nightgown out of this drawer last night, and the picture hadn't been there. Her newfound faith in her sanity after she had talked with Drew suffered a jolt.

But she couldn't be imagining this. It was broad daylight. She had just come upstairs from talking to Portia and Aunt Winnie. Her eyes were wide open. This could not be a dream! What was going on? Was somebody in this house trying to use her clinical depression to make her doubt her sanity? But she hadn't told anyone about it except Drew. Rissa's hands clenched when she remembered how she had talked to her grandfather the day she'd sat with him. But Peg had been gone and no one else had been on the third floor. Was Grandfather more lucid and mobile than any of them suspected? She couldn't believe that her grandfather would harm her.

Since no one except Drew actually believed that she hadn't imagined the wailing woman and the note that had disappeared as mysteriously as it had appeared, Rissa decided she wouldn't mention this photo to anyone. Whoever had put the picture there might get curious about why Rissa hadn't mentioned it and lead to a new clue in the case.

She wrapped a handkerchief around the picture to protect any lingering fingerprints. She unlocked her jewelry box, put the frame beneath her jewelry and locked the box. She usually kept this key with the other keys in her purse, but she removed it from the key ring, put it on a chain and hung it around her neck. Unless the jewelry box itself was taken, no one could make this picture do a disappearing act.

She had to conceal her inner feelings so that Portia wouldn't suspect how uneasy she was. She joined Portia in the lower hall. Arm in arm they walked back and forth along the driveway. A few birds twittered in the hedge around the gazebo.

"Did you enjoy your lunch with Mick yesterday?"

"Yes, but both of us are upset because our wedding is on hold. He wants to take off time for a honeymoon when we get married, but he won't consider going away as long as so many crimes are unsolved. He's still skeptical about the death of that private investigator, Garrett McGraw, wondering if the evidence implicating Mick's former perp of the murder was all phony. He's worried about his job if he and Drew can't learn what's going on. He won't marry me without any job security. I understand his position, but I've waited a long time for happiness."

"We could still do some preliminary shopping if you want to."

"I'll ask Mick if it's all right for us to leave for the day. But it's hard to make plans when we don't even know when Mother's funeral will be. Have you heard anything about that?"

"Aunt Winnie told me that her body has been brought to the funeral home, but it may be a week or more before we have the funeral."

"Surely that isn't right!" Portia protested. "Why wait so long? I can't stand any more delays."

Rissa said sarcastically, "There apparently isn't a casket in the state of Maine that Father thinks is appropriate for his 'beloved' wife, and he's having one made out of walnut wood that has been cut from the Blanchard forests and kiln dried. He's also having a mausoleum erected for her interment and for future Blanchards." She shuddered inwardly, thinking of being penned up in a granite tomb. But knowing that when she died, regardless of where her body was placed, she would spend eternity with God calmed her anxious thoughts.

"That makes me sick to my stomach," Portia said. "How can he be so two-faced? All of these years I've never heard a good word out of him about our mother, and he puts on this pretense after she's gone." She lowered her voice. "The way he's carrying on makes me wonder if he really *did* kill her and he thinks he won't be suspected if he acts like the grieving widower."

"Don't even think it! I couldn't bear to learn that Father had deliberately killed Mother."

"I know what you mean, but in some ways he had already killed her for us by pretending all of these years that she had died."

"Have you ever been sorry you were born a Blanchard?" Rissa asked, slanting a pensive look toward her twin.

"More times than I can count on ten fingers at least."

"Well, we can't change our past, but I pray that I'll have the courage in the future to forget I'm a Blanchard and try to find some happiness in life."

As she spoke, Rissa wondered what it would take to make her satisfied with her life. She had thought success in her career would be the ultimate happiness. But now that she could be considered a successful playwright, something still seemed to be missing.

Suddenly Rissa thought of Drew and how quickly their slight acquaintance had turned into friendship. Or was it more than friendship? Did her future depend on a deeper relationship with Drew?

NINE

Rissa supposed that she would always have lapses when she wondered about the extent of her depression. As soon as she went to her room after her walk, she checked to see if the picture was still in her jewelry box. Hallelujah! The picture *was* there. She felt a satisfied smile spread across her face.

She studied her mother's face, trying to connect it to the face of the woman who'd been murdered in the library. Tears stung her eyes as she mourned the mother she had never known. She hurriedly dropped the picture in its hiding place and locked the jewelry box when she heard Portia's footsteps approaching.

"I suppose it's out of the question to go to Portland to shop, but let's at least go into town tomorrow," Portia said. "Peg told me there's a card shop on Beaumont Avenue that carries a lot of wedding supplies, like invitations, favors and all. We can check that out."

"I'd like to do that," Rissa said. "I need to stop in the drugstore for a few things."

She wouldn't tell Portia that she had mislaid her prescription, because it was easier for her if no one knew about her depression. She always kept it in her purse rather than on a dresser or in the bathroom. She didn't know how it could have disappeared out of her purse. And it worried her that some member of the family would find the bottle before she did. Fortunately, she had just gotten an extended prescription before she'd left New York, and she would have no trouble getting a refill in Stoneley.

Since Ronald didn't go out that evening, Rissa didn't dare spend much time with Drew. As soon as Ronald went into his office after dinner, Rissa approached Drew, who sat in a chair near the entryway where he could see the staircase, the upstairs hallway and entrances to some of the rooms.

"I'll say good-night now."

"I'm taking twenty-four hours off starting tomorrow morning. Another officer will be on duty, so don't be afraid."

"I feel safer if you're here, but I know you need time off. Portia and I are coming into town tomorrow for the same reason. For one thing, I've lost my medication and I need to get another bottle of it."

"If you aren't able to sleep without it, I'll be here if you want someone to talk to."

"Oh. I have a few pills left. Right now, I feel more relaxed than I've felt for several days."

He pushed himself into a standing position, and his eyes caught and held hers. Without touching her, he leaned forward and brushed a gentle kiss across Rissa's lips. His lips were warm and sweet on hers. She caressed his cheek before she turned and walked swiftly upstairs.

Rissa didn't know how long she would have slept the next morning if Portia hadn't nudged her at seven o'clock.

"Hey, twin," she said. "Breakfast is in a half hour. You'd better rise and shine!" Portia drew open the draperies and sunlight flooded the room.

Rissa pulled a blanket over her head to shield her eyes from the light.

"Come on," Portia said, pulling back the covers. "Miranda and I have both finished in the bathroom. Hurry!"

"I feel like a new person this morning. I haven't rested much since I got home," she said, wondering how much Drew's kiss had to do with her improved vitality.

She walked to the window and opened it, inhaling deeply of the breeze from the ocean. "It looks like this will be a beautiful day. Let's concentrate on enjoying it, instead of dwelling on what's been happening."

"I'm with you. We'll leave for town as soon as Father goes to work. I'm sure he would forbid us leaving the property, but I can't see that we're showing any more disrespect by going shopping and to lunch than he is when he's going to work."

It was half-past ten before Rissa and Portia started for Stoneley, with Portia seething because the officer at the gate wouldn't let them leave until he okayed it with Mick.

Portia insisted on driving her vintage VW rather than riding in Rissa's Porsche, saying that she had to get used to the kind of life she would live as the wife of a small-town police detective. "All of us can't live like successful playwrights."

"Stop teasing me. I feel at peace with the world this morning, and I don't want to be pestered."

Portia laughed as she whizzed past the guard at the gate, and Rissa didn't know if she was laughing at him or at her.

The VW might have been old but it was fast, and the town of Stoneley soon came into sight.

When she had graduated from high school, Rissa couldn't wait to see the last of Stoneley, but she had to admit that the town was remarkable for its picturesque harbors and the rugged peninsulas that provided breathtaking scenery. Not far offshore was a nineteenth-century lighthouse that still protected mariners along the coast of Maine.

Although tourists had thronged the streets during the Winter Festival in February, usually throughout the rest of the winter Stoneley didn't get many visitors. But the springlike weather must have enticed them to visit today because Portia had trouble finding a parking place. She crawled along Pine Street and luckily found an empty space just a few doors from the card shop where she wanted to shop for wedding favors and invitations.

"You go on in the card shop and look around," Rissa said. "I have to buy a few items, so it may be a while before I join you."

The pharmacist said he could fill the prescription within fifteen or twenty minutes, so Rissa wandered up and down the aisles of the store while she waited. She ran into Barbara Sanchez, her father's executive assistant, when she turned up an aisle.

"Hello," Barbara said, and Rissa greeted her warmly.

A widow in her forties with two children, Barbara had worked at Blanchard Fabrics for years and seemed almost part of the family. Barbara and her family were always invited to important events at Blanchard Manor, and Rissa had often heard her father say that he couldn't run the business without Barbara. Her mixed heritage was evident in her olive skin and ebony eyes that she'd gotten from her Hispanic father.

Her eyes were compassionate as she took one of Rissa's hands in her own. "I'm so sorry for all of you, and I want you to know that you're constantly in my prayers."

After thanking Barbara for her condolences, Rissa said, "I suppose I'm still in shock. It's difficult for me to comprehend what has happened. I'd believed for years that my mother was dead. Then a few weeks ago we were told that she was alive, and now she *is* dead."

"I hope you won't blame your father too much for what he did. He was only trying to protect you. Poor man! He goes around the office like he's in another world. Working so closely with him all of these years, I've known that he has always been in love with his wife. I've heard from Winnie that she was a lovely person. I can understand why he felt that way."

Through the years, Rissa had heard suggestions that more than a business relationship was between her father and Barbara. Rissa had never noticed any sign of this when Barbara and Ronald were together. Now, considering Barbara's reaction to Trudy's death, she discounted the suggestion as a groundless rumor and nothing more.

The pharmacist called her name over the intercom. Rissa thanked Barbara for her kind words and went to pick up the prescription. As she left the pharmacy, she wondered again what could have happened to the medication she had brought from the city.

When she reached the card shop, Portia was sitting at a table with a humongous book in front of her. "They don't have much in stock, but they can order anything in this catalog."

She pushed another large book across the table to Rissa. "That catalog is from a different company. You check through it and see if you find anything interesting. Then we can compare notes."

Weddings hadn't been a part of Rissa's life. Delia was the only one of the sisters who'd gotten married, but that had been an underage elopement, which her father had annulled. She had no idea how to plan a wedding, but she did what Portia asked and dutifully turned the large pages, making a list of items and where they could be found.

After Rissa closed the book, Portia asked, "Have you found any good ideas?"

"There are several pretty invitations and napkin samples. Some of the favors are clever—bags of birdseed to throw instead of rice, small bottles of bubbles to shower on the bride and groom when they leave the church. And there are some wrappers with the bride and groom's names printed on them, which can be put around candy bars and given as favors to the guests."

"I've seen several clever gift ideas, too. My mind is completely muddled."

The proprietor must have heard them talking, because she stopped by the table. "Most people look through our books to see what's available and come back later to place their orders after they've have time to consider all their options."

Giving the woman a wide smile, Portia closed the book and stood. "That's what we'll do. But thanks for letting us look."

Leaving the card shop, Portia looked at her watch. "I told Mick we would meet him at the Clam Bake Café. It's only a short walk, so let's leave the car parked here."

They reached the café in a few minutes. A police cruiser was parked in front.

"Mick is on time for a change," Portia said. "That's one bad thing about dating a police officer—you never know whether he'll be able to keep a date. I can't imagine what it will be like to be married to one. Mick is married to his job, too, so I hope I don't come in second place most of the time."

"I'm sure he'll find time for you," Rissa said. The thought crossed her mind that a woman who married Drew would have the same problem. "There must be a lot of downtime in a small place like Stoneley."

"I'm sure there is. I just happened to become engaged

to Mick when a crime wave came along involving the Blanchard family."

Portia pushed open the door to the café, and Rissa was impressed by the bright, airy dining room.

"I believe my fiancé already has a table," Portia said to the hostess. Delighted by the nautical decor of the restaurant, Rissa paused inside the door, looking at a large mural of a fleet of fishing boats. She considered the picture a fitting tribute to the industry that had been important to Stoneley since its founding in the seventeenth century. She had just discovered that the nautical theme was carried out in the tables shaped like captain's wheels, when Portia said, "Well, well! Mick brought a guest with him."

Portia slanted an amused glance toward Rissa, who looked up quickly. Drew sat at the table with Mick. Rissa's pulse accelerated, but she hoped her inner feelings weren't apparent. In spite of her resolve, however, she felt her face getting warm, and she thought of the kiss they'd shared last night.

Both men stood, and Mick said, "You know Drew, don't you, Rissa?"

"How could I have avoided it when he's been underfoot for the past few days?" she said, smiling to take the sting out of her words. "But it's been comforting to have him on guard."

She reached across the table and shook hands with him as though they were casual acquaintances rather than close confidants. "Can't you escape the Blanchards on your day off?"

"He didn't try very hard," Mick said. "I only had to twist his arm a time or two to get him to join us."

The waitress hovered nearby with menus and the four of them sat down. After they gave their beverage orders, Rissa said to the waitress, "Give us a few minutes, will you? This is my first time here, and I want to check out all the entrées before I order."

"Let's not talk about the murder while we eat," Portia said.

"Suits me to a T," Mick said. "I'd like to escape it for a little while."

Because the other three had eaten at the café many times, they suggested their favorites to Rissa.

She listened to their comments, but she said, "I noticed none of you mentioned the blackened shrimp Caesar salad. I've had that a few times in the city. That's what I want."

"It's only been added to the menu recently," Drew said. "It sounded spicy to me and I wasn't interested in it. But since you recommend it, I'll order that."

"If you don't like hot dishes, maybe you'd better not. It has Cajun spice in it."

"I'll risk it," Drew said. He gave his order to the waitress, adding, "I want a *big* glass of water, just in case."

Portia and Mick also ordered the salad. They nibbled on crackers and talked about Mick's work with the youth group at Unity Christian Church while they waited to be served. In a short while the waitress brought their order.

Mick protested loudly when he took the first

mouthful of the spicy Caesar salad, and he downed half a glass of ice water. Rissa couldn't tell if the food was too hot for him or if he was joshing her. But her companions must have enjoyed the salad as much as she did, because they ate everything but the bowls.

For a short time Rissa was able to forget her nightmares, her depression and the unhappy situation surrounding her family. She listened eagerly to the others chatting about the everyday life of Stoneley—the way the shops were gearing up for the tourist season and the efforts of the local merchants to retain the atmosphere of the past.

Rissa thought about her childhood, when it had been an adventure to visit the five-and-dime store, the general stores and the old-fashioned movie house where Aunt Winnie had often brought her and Portia. She had been eager to leave this area, and she would never want to live here again. In fact, she couldn't imagine how Portia, after living in the city for four years, could actually be happy to return to the slow pace of Stoneley.

"Hey!" Mick said. "We aren't giving Rissa equal time. It's your time to talk. Tell us about your hectic life in New York."

"Unless you've lived in a large city, you wouldn't know that you're actually more alone in New York than you are here in Stoneley. I walk along the streets crowded with hundreds of pedestrians for days on end and never see a familiar face. I have my own small circle of friends and we keep in touch, often by e-mail, but I like the privacy of a city."

"It would suffocate me to be among so many people," Mick said. "I like the wide, open spaces."

"Not me," Drew said. "I've always lived in places where my life is an open book for everybody in town to read—where everybody not only knows their neighbors' business, but makes it theirs, as well. It can get a little tiring having few personal secrets. New York sounds like my kind of city. Tell us some more."

Rissa wasn't always comfortable talking about herself, but she could tell that Drew was interested.

"When I'm working on a new play, or have a deadline to meet, I might spend a week or two in my apartment without going out. When Portia lived with me, we would have dinner together, but she spent long hours in her shop so I had the apartment to myself.

"Sometimes I spend the day in Manhattan, ogling the skyscrapers like a tourist. It still amazes me how many people pour off and on the subways, especially at the beginning of the workday or the evening rush, when workers who live in the suburbs head home."

Drew knew instinctively as Rissa talked about her lifestyle that she was no longer sitting in a tiny café in a remote section of Maine. Her thoughts transported her to a place she loved and where she would always want to live. That fact would be of prime importance to him, *if* he were considering a relationship with Rissa, but he put a halt to his thoughts. Rissa Blanchard could never be a part of his future, and he had to realize that before his heart got completely involved.

Still thinking of her city life, Rissa said, "When my

creativity needs stimulation, I spend the day wandering around Central Park, observing all the people I see. I'm inspired when I see people of all ages walking, playing musical instruments for handouts, or watching artists draw pictures in front of my eyes. I particularly enjoy watching families having a good time."

She shook her head. "Sorry, I didn't mean to bore you. As you might guess, I'm eager to go home."

It was obvious to Drew that Blanchard Manor would never be "home" to Rissa again.

"Hey!" he protested. "Who said we were bored?"

"No, I'd like to hear more," Mick said, "but we have to go. Thanks for helping two lonely cops forget their problems for a while."

Driving back home, Portia slanted a curious glance toward her twin. "Do you like Drew?"

Without meeting her sister's eyes, Rissa said, "I have certainly liked having him around the house for protection the past few days. But I hardly know him. Give me a break, twin! Just because you're jumping into marriage, don't expect me to do the same. I'm married to my profession—you know that."

"Maybe," Portia said skeptically. "But I think Drew likes you."

Her sister's words served as a stimulant to Rissa's jumbled emotions but she didn't answer.

Humming contentedly, Rissa climbed the stairs at Portia's side.

"I want to get Miranda's opinion about a scarf to wear to the funeral. I'll be back soon," Portia said.

Rissa entered the bedroom feeling better than she had since she'd found her mother's body. She opened her dresser drawer to put away the few purchases she had made in the drugstore. Her contentment faded immediately.

The picture of her mother, Portia and herself had disappeared. In its place was a picture of a tombstone.

Rissa knew then that her troubles were not over. What would happen next?

TEN

Rissa heard Portia's steps behind her. She piled some garments over the picture and quickly closed the dresser drawer. Her heart pounded in her chest and she struggled to catch her breath. She kept her face hidden so Portia wouldn't notice her discomfiture.

"Miranda wasn't in her room," Portia said, "but Aunt Winnie waved to me, and she wants to see us." Portia led the way down the hall where their aunt waited by the door of her room. The expression on Aunt Winnie's face did not indicate good news.

Miranda was slumped in a chair upholstered in white fabric. Her eyes glistened with tears and she twisted a handkerchief in her hand.

"Now what?" Rissa said as Aunt Winnie motioned them to sit on a couch that was upholstered in bright floral fabric.

"You'll never believe what your father is proposing now."

"Try me," Rissa said. "I wouldn't put anything past Father."

"Sit down," Aunt Winnie said. "Towering over me like you are makes me more nervous than I am already."

Rissa and Portia exchanged sharp glances, and they sat side by side on the couch.

"He's turning Trudy's funeral into a big spectacle. He's proposing to have her body here in the house for viewing. He intends to hold the funeral in the country club because it's more roomy than the church. And in his opinion, there's no minister in Stoneley with enough dignity to conduct a worthy funeral for Trudy. He's having a more prominent preacher come from Portland."

"But we have such a small family," Miranda wailed. "We don't need a large place."

"There may not be many mourners," Winnie said, "but there will be a large crowd. Curiosity, if no other reason, will prompt the local residents to see the Blanchard family on display."

"I agree there will be a lot of people if it's an open funeral," Rissa said. "We have to remember how many people around here owe their jobs to the Blanchards, and they won't want to offend Father. I'm for having a private funeral—family members only. As far as I'm concerned, it's time for someone to stand up to Father. He can disinherit me if he wants to, but I will not attend a funeral at the country club, and if he makes a public display by bringing our mother's body here, I'm going back to the city."

"You're the main witness to this murder," Miranda reminded her. "The police won't let you go away."

Rissa hoped that, with Drew on the force, the authorities wouldn't detain her. "They will unless they put me in jail, and in that case, I still won't have to be involved in any of this foolishness."

"I feel the same way," Portia said, snuggling close to Rissa. The twins had often presented a united front to the rest of the family.

"Then shall we meet with your father and tell him our sentiments?" Winnie asked.

"The sooner the better," Rissa said.

"But one thing bothers me. I don't mind if the funeral is public, but I would like to have it in the church," Winnie said. "If we agree that the body can be in the church for an hour, he might agree to the memorial service. Your father won't be easily intimidated, so we may have to compromise."

"Is he home now?" Rissa asked.

"Yes, in his office, of course," Miranda said.

"Then let's go down and lay our cards on the table. I don't like to prolong unpleasant situations," Rissa said.

The four women walked downstairs two abreast like a trained army going to war. Their brave stance dissipated somewhat when they reached the office door. Everyone hesitated, and summoning her courage, Rissa stepped forward and knocked forcefully.

"Who is it?" Ronald growled.

Without answering, Rissa opened the door and walked inside, with the others crowding close behind her. She stopped in amazement when she saw a wedding picture of her parents prominently displayed on Ronald's desk.

"What do you want?" he said, quickly turning the picture facedown.

"We want to talk with you about the funeral. Do you think it's your right to make all the plans without considering our wishes at all?" Rissa demanded.

"I do what I want to do."

"We're aware of that, and I suppose I'm just like you. For in this matter, I intend to do what *I* want to do."

"Such as?" Ronald said, sneering.

"Unless you stop all of this ostentation and plan a private funeral, I'm leaving for the city as soon as possible."

"We all feel this way, Ronald." Winnie tried to reason with her brother. "We won't go to the country club nor do we want another preacher brought in. I believe the service should be held in Unity Christian Church with Reverend Brown in charge."

"This is *my* household, and you'll do what *I* say."

Rissa was surprised when Miranda defied her father. "This isn't the Dark Ages, where men owned the women of their family body and soul. We're not slaves anymore. In case you haven't heard, women have been liberated. You've already hurt us enough by telling us that our mother was dead when you knew very well that she wasn't. Can't we at least have a decent funeral to mourn her passing?"

"I wash my hands of the lot of you. Don't you think I'm grieving, too?"

Rissa shook her head negatively, and she sensed that Aunt Winnie and her sisters did the same. A look of guilt flitted momentarily across Ronald's face.

"Have you considered," Winnie said, "that this lavish display of grief will only confirm in the public's mind that a member of this family killed Trudy and that we're trying to cover it up?"

Ronald's head came up as if he had been stung, as if the thought hadn't occurred to him. He still didn't give up easily, but wrangled with them for an hour over minor issues. At last they compromised. Trudy's body would be in the funeral home for viewing, but the family would have a private viewing. She would be buried in the hand-crafted casket in the mausoleum. The funeral would be public but held at Unity Christian Church with Reverend Brown in charge. The family wouldn't be required to wear black to the funeral and the notice in the paper would ask that in lieu of flowers, memorials would be sent to Unity Christian Church for the youth program.

"When are the rest of the girls coming home?" Ronald asked.

"Juliet's conference ends tonight and she'll be home tomorrow. Bianca will come the day before the funeral. Delia will book her flight as soon as she knows when the funeral will be, but she plans to return to Hawaii immediately after the memorial service. She's been away from her business too much since the first of the year."

"We will set the funeral for a week from today. I'll contact the funeral home," Ronald said.

As they left the room, Rissa exchanged skeptical glances with her twin. Their father had capitulated too easily. Did that mean they could still expect trouble from him? Or was he responsible for Trudy's death and conceding because he worried that an overt display of grief would cast suspicion on him?

Drew believed that Rissa reciprocated his feelings and was somehow put off by his reticence.

That night Ronald went out, presumably to spend the evening with Alannah Stafford. Drew wondered if Rissa might come downstairs after her father left.

Since he didn't want to put Rissa in a compromising situation, and realizing that he wouldn't be privy to what was happening in the house if he was inside the living room, he sat on the bench in the hallway.

As soon as Rissa heard her father drive away, she left Portia in their room talking on the phone with Mick. She was eager to talk to Drew about the confrontation with their father.

"You've finished your dinner already?" she asked Drew when she approached him in the hallway.

"After our big lunch, I'm going to settle for a midnight snack."

"Is it all right if I keep you company? Or, I'll be honest, you'd be keeping me company. Portia is talking to Mick, and Aunt Winnie and Miranda are watching television in the sitting room while waiting to get a call through to our sister Delia in Hawaii."

"I'll bring a chair from the living room," he said. "Except for this bench, none of the other furniture looks too comfortable, and I need to sit here to monitor who comes and goes."

"Most of this furniture is from another century and it isn't comfortable. Not much changes at Blanchard Manor, except the people."

He picked up a platform rocker and carried it to a place near the bench.

"When is the funeral scheduled?"

"A week from today. The mausoleum won't be ready until then. Aunt Winnie, my sisters and I had a royal battle with Father this afternoon about the funeral. He was determined to make a big show and we didn't want it. I was ready to go back to the city if he persisted in his plans, but Miranda said I wouldn't be allowed to leave Stoneley because I'm the only witness to my mother's murder."

"Mick and I would consider making an exception in your case and perhaps allow you to go home while we continue the investigation. To be honest, I'm uneasy about having you here. That note you received has me wondering if the killer thought you could identify him. Or her," he amended. "And those nightmares you've been having could have been triggered by someone who wants you to think you're losing your mind."

"But how could anyone do that?"

"I don't know." He moved his shoulders in a shrug of defeat. "They could have your bedroom bugged. Or if someone in this house is the murderer, that person might have learned the kind of antidepressants you're taking and have slipped you something else to counteract your medication. And you haven't told anyone that you're taking an antidepressant?"

"No," Rissa said, and stopped suddenly, remembering. "I did tell Grandfather, but only the two of us were in his apartment, and he didn't pay any attention to me at all—he was off in a little world of his own."

"He might have heard you, but in his condition, he couldn't be harassing you. Didn't you say a bottle of your pills had disappeared?"

"They're gone, but I've probably just misplaced them. No one except you knows about my depression, and none of the family would have any idea what would cause me to hallucinate."

"They would if they saw what your prescription is. I'm trying to look at every angle of this situation, and we can't overlook the fact that if someone other than a resident of Blanchard Manor killed your mother, they had to get in the house some way. Do all of the servants have a code to get through the gate and into the house?"

"The ones who live here in the house would have. I'm not sure anyone else would know it. But I haven't had any nightmares for a couple of nights now."

"I only hope that continues. But be careful. It might be a good idea to lock your bedroom door at night."

In an attempt to turn the conversation to a lighter subject, Rissa said, "You know so much about my family, and I hardly know anything about yours...."

Rissa was sorry immediately that she had asked and wished that she could recall the words.

Drew, on the other hand, was pleased that she had led into the subject he knew had to be addressed.

"As I mentioned the other night, my dad was an

abusive man, not only to my mother, but to me. He'd beat up on me for no apparent reason. I couldn't do much about it until I was a teenager. By that time I was taller than he was and heavier. When I turned fifteen, I'd had all I intended to take, and when he hit my mother, I attacked him. He was drinking, and I suppose I took an unfair advantage of him, but I gave him a bad beating. When I finished, I told my mother she could either kick him out or I was leaving for good. That goaded her into divorcing him and he disappeared from our lives."

"I shouldn't have asked. This is obviously very painful for you."

"No, I've wanted to tell you more about what happened with my father. You need to understand how different we are. You grew up in this—" he waved a hand indicating the opulence of Blanchard Manor "—and I lived in a rented house, not as good as the outbuildings on this property. You're heir to a lot of wealth, and I don't own anything except a pickup truck. Our worlds are miles part."

"Do you think that makes any difference to me?" she whispered.

Their glances locked and fierce emotion pierced Rissa's heart. Drew must have experienced the same thing, for he reached his hand toward her, but drew it back immediately. He stood and walked to the rear of the hallway, checking the rooms as if nothing had happened. But Rissa knew better. They were intimately aware of each other and she wondered what might happen if she made more than an overture of friendliness to Drew.

After the tumultuous romantic affairs of her father, Rissa had steered clear of relationships during her teen years and in college. After going to New York, her only passion was to succeed as a playwright. Now she wondered if that was enough. Knowing that it wasn't, she went back to her room before Drew finished checking the manor. Every night he was sure that all the doors were locked and that the security system was activated. Once again she asked herself how anyone could have possibly slipped into the house to kill Trudy.

Rissa's mind was troubled when she tried to sleep.

At breakfast the next morning, Winnie said, "Juliet called last night and she'll arrive at the Portland airport at two o'clock today. I'm going to meet her, but the rest of you are welcome to go, too. Poor child—she's going to need all the love we can give her."

"But it should be some comfort for her to know that she wasn't responsible for her mother's death as she's always thought."

Rissa had never been able to understand Juliet's reasoning on that issue. Just because her mother's mental condition stemmed from postpartum syndrome, it wasn't Juliet's fault. She hadn't asked to be born.

"I'll go with you, Auntie. Do you want to go, twin?" Portia asked.

"No, I'll stay here."

Rissa wanted to stay behind hoping to have a few

hours alone with Drew. Only the household staff and Miranda would be left in the house. Since Trudy's murder, Miranda avoided the front part of the house as much as possible. Except when she came down the back stairs to the dining room, she stayed on the second floor.

By the time Winnie and Portia were ready to leave, a quick shower had blown in from the ocean and the pavement was still wet. Rissa stepped out on the porch to say goodbye as the limousine was driven away by the chauffeur. When she returned to the foyer and closed the door, Drew was coming down the steps with a duffel bag.

"Oh, you're leaving, too?" Rissa asked, trying to stifle the disappointment in her voice.

"Just for a few hours," he answered. "Mick is sending an officer to fill in for me, and I'm going home to check on things. Who else is gone?"

"Aunt Winnie and Portia went to the airport to meet Juliet. She's flying in from Florida."

Wondering if he had lost his senses, Drew said, "Do you want to come with me? I've seen your home—you might as well see mine."

"Will the officer let me leave the property without a lot of explanations?"

"They won't ask any questions if you're with me. I'll bring you home when you're ready."

"It will probably be two or three hours before the others are back, so I will go with you. It's such a pretty day and I don't want to be penned up inside. Give me a minute to get a jacket and tell someone where I'm going."

Pleasure lent speed to her feet as she all but danced

up the steps. When she reached the second floor, Sonya was plodding down the hall on her daily inspection of the house, insuring that the maids had done their work satisfactorily.

"Sonya, I'm going out for a couple of hours with Detective Lancaster. If Aunt Winnie gets back before I do, please tell her that I'll be back before too long."

"Will do," Sonya said. "You're looking peaked. You need to get out of this house. Have fun."

Rissa searched her closet and pulled the brown leather jacket she had bought in a classy boutique on Fifth Avenue over her shoulders. She had left the jacket behind the last time she'd been home. She kicked off her chic stacked-heel sandals and slid her feet into a pair of flats.

Remembering what Sonya had said about looking peaked, she scanned her face, not really liking what she saw. Rissa had often wished she could change her dark features for Juliet's long blond hair and fair complexion. Shrugging off a phenomenon that she knew could never happen she ran down the steps, excited that she and Drew could have a short time outside the gloomy atmosphere of the manor.

His replacement had arrived, and Drew waited for her in the foyer. She felt giddy, as if she were a teenager going on her first date. He held the door open for her and she sensed that he was as thrilled about their outing as she was.

After they left the Blanchard property, Drew followed the road along the coastline—one of Rissa's favorite drives—which bypassed the town of Stoneley.

She lowered the window a notch and listened to the splash of the surf against the rocky coast. Huge spruce trees glistened with some remaining drizzle as shafts of sunshine streamed through the clouds. The sky, which had been drab and gray when they'd left the house, had broken into patches of dazzling white.

This was the first time they had been completely alone and Rissa didn't know what to say. Drew was equally silent.

She hesitated to break the mood, which she considered peaceful, but she finally said, "It's good to be away for a little while and not feel like a cloud is hanging over my head ready to fall on me. Thanks for bringing me along."

"I enjoy being with you, in case you haven't noticed," he commented wryly.

She glanced his way, and he gave her a smile that set her pulse racing. She immediately looked away toward the ocean. "Maybe I have noticed, because I like being with you, too."

"We live in two different worlds, Rissa."

"We both live in Maine," she answered teasingly.

"Rich and poor don't mix. They never have—never will."

"I'm far from rich. It's expensive to live in New York. You probably have more in your bank account than I have in mine."

"But you know where you could get a lot of money if you need it. That makes a difference," he reminded her.

"Let's not spoil our few hours together arguing about our differences. That won't change things."

"I guess you're right."

Drew left the coastal road and turned upward toward several scattered houses perched on a rugged peninsula. He pulled into the driveway of a cottage, and Rissa noticed at once that it needed a coat of paint.

"This is home, sweet home for me. Come in."

They climbed three steps to a narrow covered porch.

"Who is it? Who is it?" someone screeched as soon as Drew unlocked the door.

Rissa stopped abruptly and looked at Drew, reassured by the smile on his face.

"Come in and meet Rudolph."

ELEVEN

He held the door for her and Rissa stepped into Drew's living room. A blue-and-green parrot blinked at them from the security of a large cage. "We've got company, Rudolph. Come out and meet the lady." He opened the cage door.

"Squawk," the parrot answered, ruffling his feathers and turning his back on Drew.

"Ignore him. He'll come out soon enough."

Half-afraid of the parrot's beady eyes and large beak, Rissa took Drew's advice.

With a sweeping arm, Drew snagged her attention and she stopped watching the parrot.

"So you see where I live. We're in the combination living room and kitchen now. My bedroom and hobby room are in the back. Not a very pretentious home, is it?"

Rissa looked around the area. She had never seen any house so lacking in the comforts of home. Was this the way Drew preferred to live…or couldn't he afford anything better? She knew she hadn't concealed her horror from Drew, because he laughed.

"I didn't figure you'd like my home."

"There isn't anything wrong with the house except there isn't anything in it," she answered. "You don't have any curtains or blinds."

The hardwood floor had no carpet, not even a throw rug. His furniture consisted of a plastic-covered lounge chair parked in front of a medium-size television. A matching couch was located along the bedroom wall, but it was covered with magazines. Where else would he have put them? There wasn't a table in the living area.

She muddled her way into the middle of the kitchen, unnerved by the starkness of her surroundings. There was a built-in sink, a refrigerator, a small range and a table with two folding chairs that had probably been there since the house had been built at least thirty years ago. An open door revealed a pantry. Drew leaned against the modern refrigerator while she gazed from one appliance to another.

Hearing a whirring sound next to her ears, she flinched as Rudolph landed on her shoulders.

"Oh!" she said and swatted at the parrot.

"Squawk." Rudolph screeched, pecked her on the head, left her shoulder and landed on top of Drew's head. He stared at her and clacked his beak.

Rissa collapsed into one of the chairs and tried to regain her composure. Drew took the parrot from his shoulder and tossed him toward the cage. Screeching, "Stop! Stop!" the parrot whizzed into the cage and pulled the door shut behind him.

Drew knelt beside Rissa. "Did he hurt you?"

She shook her head and clenched her hands together. Too late, Drew decided that he had gone overboard in his effort to show Rissa that their worlds didn't mix.

She covered her face with her hands, ashamed of her reaction to the parrot, but the bird had surprised her, which was more than her taut nerves could handle. She had already been on the verge of tears, shocked at Drew's apparent content with his poor living conditions.

"Why do you live like this?" she asked. "And don't tell me you can't afford anything better. Portia told me how much Mick makes."

He went to the sink, washed his hands and took a bottle of cola from the refrigerator. He filled two plastic cups with chipped ice and poured some of the cola over it. He gave one of the cups to her and she took a big swallow.

"The house I lived in when I was a kid wasn't much better than this," Drew said softly, trying to soften her shock at his austere surroundings. "My mother does live more comfortably now that she's alone. I give her some financial help, too. And you're right—I could live better than this, but why? I'd rather save my money. I don't expect to stay a small-town cop all of my life. A bank account is my meal ticket to something better."

"It isn't my business, anyway, and I apologize for saying anything. The place seemed so bare, and I felt bad that you have to live here and then that parrot scared me. Forgive me?"

"Sure!" he said, raising his cup to her. "I'd forgotten about Rudolph until we started in the house or I'd have warned you."

"Where'd you get him?"

"He belonged to an old seaman who lived in this house, but who died before I moved in. I rent the house from the man's sister, and Rudolph sort of went with the place. I put up with him because it's kinda nice to have something to come home to even if it is only a parrot."

She finished her cola and set the cup on the table.

"Do you want me to fill it again?"

"No, thanks."

He dumped the ice into the sink and dropped the cups in a waste can. "Come into another room—I think you'll like it there."

He put his arm around her shoulders and steered her toward the bedroom area.

"I really should be leaving," she said, suddenly feeling ill at ease. Even though Drew was a cop and she had faith in him, the truth was that they barely knew each other and she'd be wise to keep her guard up. "I want to be home when my family gets back from the airport."

Perhaps sensing the reason for her hesitation, Drew turned her gently to face him. "I don't want you to leave with a negative attitude. Trust me! This won't take long."

She searched his eyes for a moment. She knew instinctively that her reaction to his plea for trust would determine their future relationship—for good or bad. She yielded to his suggestion by moving forward. He tightened his embrace briefly and released her.

They walked down a short hallway facing a bathroom. Drew's bedroom was to the left, and although it was as stark in appearance as the rest of the house, the bed was neatly made. Rissa experienced an inner sigh of relief when Drew turned toward the closed door to the right. He unlocked the door, turned on a light and stepped back for Rissa to enter first. To leave the simply furnished part of Drew's home for his workshop was like entering a new world.

The room was brilliantly lit with several strips of fluorescent lights. Numerous model airplanes hung from the ceiling. Shelves along the walls contained model airplanes of all sizes. A large worktable, holding a skeleton replica of an antique plane, dominated the center of the room. Speechless, Rissa pivoted and surveyed the room from all angles.

Several dioramas depicted planes. One looked like a navy craft that had been shot down and was slowly sinking into the sea. Another plane had crashed in a desert area, so skillfully made that it seemed like the real thing. The room was a veritable museum.

Drew watched her closely, apparently intent on her reaction. Rissa's throat was so tight she couldn't speak, but she held out her left hand, and he grasped it, squeezing so tightly that she almost cried out in pain. She wiggled her fingers and he relaxed his grip.

"And you've done all of these," she murmured.

"Yes. This is the reason I haven't made my house more livable. The other rooms are just a place to eat and sleep. When I'm not at work, I spend all of my time in here."

"I want to come back when I have more time so you can tell me about all this. But give me a brief tour now.

How did you get interested in this hobby? How long have you been making planes?"

Still holding her hand, he walked to one of the shelves and picked up a replica. "This is the first plane I made. It's a World War II B-25 bomber." With a faraway look in his eyes, he continued, "I only have one pleasant memory of my father, and this is it." He handed the plane to Rissa and she held it as carefully as she would have a priceless jewel.

He sauntered to the worktable, lifted a piece of sandpaper and applied it to the wing of the model on the table. As he sanded, he said, "My father bought that kit for me when I was ten years old during one of the periods when he was trying get clean. He helped me put the model together."

When he paused for a short time, Rissa said, "And you've enjoyed the hobby ever since?"

He laid down the sandpaper, took the model plane from Rissa and put it back on the wad of modeling clay that held it in place on the shelf.

"No. He was back to his old self soon after that, and I hid the plane away for years. When I was in high school, though, I took a hobby class in vocational training and my interest in planes revived. I didn't have much room in my mother's home, so I worked in an outbuilding and kept the models packed away. When I had a place of my own, I still didn't have much room until I moved into this house. I didn't need an extra bedroom, so I remodeled this room into a workshop."

"I'm *really* impressed with what you've done. Tell me just a few things before we have to leave."

"There are thousands and thousands of kits available—probably one or more for every plane ever made, so I knew I had to specialize. Most of my models are World War II vintage. I'll just mention the ones hanging from the ceiling."

He pointed out and explained briefly the merits of a P-51 Mustang Glamorous Glen III aircraft. A P-51 Black Widow. A Japanese Zero Gray Saboru Sakai. A TBF-TBM-3 Avenger. A P-38J Lightning with Shark Teeth. And a P-40B Tomahawk.

Rissa exclaimed over each one, appreciating the talent he displayed.

"Really, it isn't hard," he said modestly. "I buy kits that have all the parts. All I have to do is follow instructions."

"All the same, you must have an aptitude for this kind of work. And it must take a lot of patience."

"It's therapy for me. I come here, close the door and forget my worries. We don't often have to deal with crimes like the ones at Blanchard Manor, but still, detective work is demanding. I can get away from everything in here."

He turned off the lights and closed the door, leaving the pleasant, well-lit room to go back to the reality of his stark existence.

"But is this all of your life?" Rissa said in bewilderment, wanting so much to understand Drew's inner self. "You work and come home. That's it? Don't you have any social life at all? No community involvement? No friends? No dates?"

With a sweeping gesture and a thin smile on his lips, he said, "This is it."

Rissa had always thought she had been deprived by a motherless childhood and without any affection from her father. But her life was wonderful when compared to Drew's. She'd had Aunt Winnie and a grandfather to love her. She had five sisters for companionship. Now she had her circle of close friends in New York. Drew had nothing but his hobby—a fact that depressed her more than it should, especially since he hadn't given her any right to enter his life.

As they walked out of the house, Rudolph screeched, "Goodbye. Goodbye."

Drew leaned against one of the porch posts and looked toward the water below them. "You asked about dating. I've avoided relationships because I don't intend to get married. It wouldn't be fair to date someone and give her false expectations. Don't you agree?"

"I suppose so," Rissa said quietly.

They drove in silence until they were a few miles from Blanchard Manor. Drew pulled to the side of the road and cleared his throat. "Since I've confided more to you this afternoon than I've ever told anyone, I might as well tell you the main reason I avoid women. Perhaps I shouldn't talk to you about such a personal matter, but I want you to know."

Rissa had already heard more than she wanted to, but she didn't comment.

"When I was taking my physicals for the police academy, I learned that I'm sterile."

She cast a surprised glance in his direction.

"I had mumps when I was a child, and as the saying

was in our town, I had a 'backset.' I'll spare you the plain facts, but it took several weeks for me to recover. I overheard my mother and another woman talking about how a backset with the mumps would keep me from fathering any children."

Rissa reached for Drew's hand and held it tightly. Sensing that this revelation was difficult for him, she said, "You don't have to tell me anything else."

Shaking his head, he said, "I want you to know. I figured it might be an old wives' tale, so when I had that physical, I asked the doctor to check my sterility. He confirmed that I couldn't father a child. Up until that time, I figured I'd get married someday, but after I learned about my physical problem, I didn't think it would be fair to a wife."

Rissa heard the defeat in his voice and she prayed for the right words to speak, but she remained silent. If anyone ever asked to marry her, she planned on being upfront about not envisioning herself as a mother. However, Drew had made it plain several times that their lives were too diverse for more than friendship. Because he hadn't given her any reason to believe that he would want to marry her despite his physical problem, she didn't feel inclined to tell him that she didn't want children.

Still trying to find words of comfort, she finally said, "I don't imagine that would matter to any woman who really loved you. If you do fall in love, shouldn't you let the woman decide?"

He gave an impatient shrug and the melancholy on his face pierced Rissa's heart.

"I just don't happen to see it that way. But that's only one of my reasons for not marrying. I don't have much to offer otherwise—no stable family background, no expectation of any wealth."

What else could she say? She'd probably already said too much. But a part of her felt like the subject remained unsettled between them.

When he pulled into the circular drive at Blanchard Manor, Rissa said, "Thanks so much for taking me to your home and sharing your enthusiasm for building model airplanes with me. I'm sorry about what you've just told me, about your physical condition. But don't worry—I won't mention it to anyone."

Rissa was alternately distressed and happy when she considered the unforgettable afternoon she'd spent with Drew. She didn't want to answer any questions about where she had been, so she was relieved that she had gotten home before her family, who arrived soon afterward.

It hadn't been long since Rissa had seen her youngest sister, Juliet, but she still hurried to meet her in the lower hall and give her a hug. In Rissa's opinion Juliet was the beauty of the family. Tall and graceful, she had long, platinum-blond hair, green eyes and fair, delicate features. Rissa had always heard that Juliet looked like their mother, and now that she had seen her mother, she recognized the close resemblance.

Juliet wore a cosmic-palette jacket with all the colors of a rainbow, a white cotton interlock T-shirt, and crosshatch jeans with sequined floral embroidery on the back pocket and lower leg. The jeans were belted with a mesh sash twinkling with coppery discs. Looking at Juliet's trendy, casual clothes, Rissa was pleased to realize that their father hadn't dampened Juliet's free spirit when she'd started working at Blanchard Fabrics.

Ronald didn't come home for dinner, and the four sisters and Winnie enjoyed a pleasant meal. Aunt Winnie and Portia had filled Juliet in on the details of the pending funeral on their way from the airport, but Winnie had forbidden any mention of the situation as they dined together.

Soon after dinner, all of them retired to their individual rooms and the house was quiet. Drew hadn't returned and another officer kept vigil in the hall below.

Rissa couldn't sleep because her mind was on the afternoon with Drew. She knew so much more about him now than she had known twenty-four hours earlier. In fact, she probably knew more about him than anyone else did. Was there any particular significance in that fact?

Could it mean that he suspected that she might have romantic feelings for him and wanted to warn her off because he wasn't interested in her? Or could it mean that he shared the same feelings that she harbored in her heart for him? If that was so, did he think it was only fair for her to know his physical limitations before their relationship intensified?

Because she was feeling cold, Rissa put on a pair of knit pajamas, slipped under the covers and turned out the light. She didn't want to keep Portia awake, and if she did leave the room, she could put a robe around her pajamas. After a half hour, it was obvious she wasn't going to sleep. She missed Drew and the security she felt when he was in the house. She realized that their nightly meetings had been the stimulant she had needed to endure the past few days.

She tried to focus on all he had going for him, but all she could think of was his defeatist attitude. He needed someone to love him and prove to him that he was important, but was she the one?

She was still awake when she heard Ronald's Jaguar pull into the driveway. A few moments later, she sighed with relief at the sound of her father's heavy tread as he climbed the steps. In spite of the police protection, she'd been afraid to leave her bedroom, but now that her father was home she felt safer. Although she harbored a suspicion that he might have killed her mother, she would never believe that he would harm one of his daughters. She recalled that as a child, she'd always felt protected when he'd been in the house. But her sense of security disappeared when a warning voice whispered in her head, "Don't forget whoever killed your mother also shot at you."

Rissa put on her slippers and robe, opened the door quietly and eased out into the corridor. She didn't want to disturb the cop in the main hallway so she padded softly toward the smaller staircase that led toward the backyard and the kitchen. She hadn't wanted much dinner and she was hungry. Andre always kept a plate of snacks available, and she thought a glass of milk and a cookie or two might help her fall asleep.

At the foot of the steps, she pulled back the curtain from a window and peered outside, wishing she dared take a walk. Today had been balmy, the first mild day Maine had experienced. Even the ocean breeze had been calm and warm. She lifted her hand to turn on the hall light to guide her to the kitchen when she heard a conversation outside. She became instantly wide awake.

The voices were muffled, but she moved close to the door and pressed her ear against the upper frosted-glass panel. She couldn't tell if the conversation was between men or women.

The tone of one voice was completely foreign to her, and she believed it was a woman talking. The other voice seemed somewhat familiar, but she couldn't hear enough to be positive. The speakers sounded as if they were several yards from the house, and to hear more easily, she decoded the security system, slid the dead bolt and turned the doorknob quietly. When the conversation continued, she cracked the door about an inch to hear more distinctly.

In the quietness of the night, although she didn't recognize the speaker, she plainly heard the words, "Are you sure she didn't recognize you?"

A guttural voice said, "My face was covered the whole time, and it was dark in the room. You worry too much."

A soft gasp escaped her when she tumbled to the fact that they were talking about her. The voices ceased abruptly and Rissa heard nothing more. Surely they couldn't have heard her. Was this another one of her delusions?

Too scared to move at first, she knew she had to return to her room. If the two people thought they had been overheard, she was in danger. Still being cautious, and in spite of her trembling, she latched the door and bolted it. She ran up the steps and into her bedroom. Her heart was racing, and groping in the darkness, she found her way to a chair.

TWELVE

Although she had taken her antidepressant after dinner, Rissa searched her purse for the medication. The psychiatrist had told her it was all right to take a double dose of the medication if she felt she needed it. She'd never been under such stress, and she hoped the tablets would calm her until she could decide what to do.

When she pulled two bottles of medicine out of her purse, Rissa paused for a moment. Had that first bottle been in her purse all along? Her mind was definitely playing tricks on her.

Rissa walked quietly to her bedside table for a glass of water to wash down the two tablets. To give time for the tablets to take effect, she walked quietly to the window that faced the backyard. She took a quick, sharp breath and shock spread throughout her body. Someone was walking through the yard toward the bluffs. Could this be one of the people she had overheard outside the back door?

Determined to find out who was loitering on the

property at night, Rissa grabbed a flashlight and her cell phone and headed downstairs. Belatedly she thought it might have been a good idea to awaken Portia and tell her what was happening, but she didn't want to upset the household unnecessarily. She stepped outside cautiously. She peered into the quiet darkness for several minutes. Seeing no one, she headed toward the cliff. She was convinced the person had taken the trail along the bluffs.

Realizing that someone needed to know what she was doing, Rissa paused near the gazebo and dialed Drew's number. He answered sleepily on the second ring.

Aware that someone might be listening, in a muted voice, she said, "I overheard two people talking outside the house tonight, and I think they were talking about me. One of them just now walked across the yard toward the bluffs. This may be the breakthrough we need. I'm going to follow and see who it is."

"No! No! Go back in the house," he ordered. "It isn't safe for you to be out."

She hung up. Refusing to heed Drew's warning, conscious only of the fact that she might be at the point of finding out who had murdered her mother, Rissa ran across the vast lawn toward the bluffs.

Partly from exertion but mostly from excitement and fear, Rissa hurried up the steep incline, thankful that it was a clear night. The revolving light from the lighthouse on the point of land opposite the bluffs provided enough light to find her way without using the flashlight. She tried to walk quietly and cringed each time she dislodged a rock that hurtled down the cliff.

She didn't see anyone ahead of her, and although she paused occasionally to listen, Rissa couldn't hear any footsteps on the trail. Anxiously, she wondered if she was hallucinating again and had imagined that someone had walked into the woods.

When she reached the highest point of the bluff, Rissa moved into the shadow of a tree and peered anxiously around her. The flashing light from the tower illuminated the bluffs for a short time—long enough for Rissa to see that the area was empty. Could the unknown individual have known that she was following?

Silence loomed around her like a heavy mist from the ocean. With the next illumination from the lighthouse, Rissa's eyes swept the pinnacle. The foolhardiness of her action stunned her. There were dozens of places where someone could be hiding—rock outcroppings, large tree trunks and underbrush. For all she knew, someone might be on a ledge below the precipice. Why hadn't she listened to Drew's insistence that she was in danger and wait for him?

She walked closer to the precipice and stopped again. All was silent except the crashing of waves on the uneven coast. The only thing to do was to call Drew and tell him she was going back to the house.

A creepy sensation crawled up Rissa's spine and she knew instinctively that someone was standing behind her. She whirled and came face-to-face with the same masked, black-robed figure that she'd seen in the library on the night her mother had been murdered.

Stunned, she backed up, stopping suddenly when

she realized how close she was to the precipice. She sidled away from the abyss and started to run. The masked person jumped toward her, lifted her in strong arms and hurled her over the yawning cliff. Her body hung suspended in space for a moment, then Rissa screamed as her body hurtled downward.

Drew heard Rissa's scream as he ground his cruiser to a sudden halt along the highway below the bluffs. He jumped from the car, and as he ran upward, he dialed Mick's number.

When Mick answered, he shouted breathlessly, "Backup! Backup needed. Rissa is in trouble. Come to the bluffs."

He dropped his phone into his pocket as he approached the precipice. He heard someone crashing through the trees and underbrush toward the coast, but he didn't follow. Rissa had been on the bluffs when she had screamed, and he surveyed the area in the faint light emanating from the lighthouse. A chilly black silence surrounded him and he couldn't control his rising panic. She wasn't anywhere to be seen.

Spurred on by his concern, he ran to the brink and looked over.

"Rissa. Rissa," he called. He listened and called again. Had he heard an answer?

"Rissa, do you hear me? Where are you?" Heedless of his own safety, he dropped to his knees and peered over.

The revolving light flickered over the cliff again just as he heard a faint "Here."

His relief was so great that he almost lost his balance and pitched headlong over the steep drop. He slid back a few inches. He was sure that he'd seen something white several feet below him. He groaned when he turned his flashlight in that direction. About six feet from the precipice, Rissa lay across the roots of two spindly evergreen trees. How could he save her before the trees bent under her weight and she plunged to a horrible death? There was a rope in the squad car, but he couldn't take time to get it.

"Stay put, sweetheart," he called. "I'll save you."

Throwing aside his jacket, Drew removed his belt, which was heavy enough to hold her, but too short to reach the ledge. He scanned the wall to the left and right of Rissa. On the right, a narrow trail provided access to a substantial ledge that was only a few feet from where she had landed.

A siren rose and fell, and he knew Mick was on his way, but Rissa's situation seemed precarious to him. Her legs hung over the abyss. Although Drew hadn't been on praying terms with God for a long time, he hadn't forgotten where to go when he needed help.

God, I've been a disobedient follower, and I don't expect You to do anything for me, but I pray for Rissa. She doesn't deserve the treatment she's received at the hand of this unknown predator. I can't do anything unless You help me.

Using his flashlight, he followed the narrow, rocky trail that led gradually downward, which brought him within a foot of the place Rissa had lodged.

"Can you move at all?" he said.

"Yes, but I'm afraid to." Her voice sounded steady in spite of the danger she faced.

Quickly unbuttoning his shirt and shrugging out of it, he said, "If you can sit up and move toward me, I'll throw my shirt to you and help you walk across to me. The ledge is too narrow for you to crawl on, but if you hold on to the shirt, I can pull you to safety if you slip."

"Drew," Mick's voice shouted, and Drew heard a sigh of relief.

"Down here," he called. "Rissa is caught in the trees, and I think I can save her on my own. But since you're here, can you get a rope?"

Mick's face peered down from above. "I'll get the rope and a harness and be back as soon as possible. Don't take any foolish risks."

Rissa was sitting up now, and Drew said, "Since Mick is bringing a rope, I'll cross to your side to help you put on the harness and he can pull you up."

"Don't do it! That ledge is too narrow for you to cross and this overhang is hardly big enough to hold me."

"I'll make it," he said. The wind was picking up now and Drew remembered that eddies sometimes developed into whirlwinds and blew up from the cove. He also knew that one false step could hurtle him to his death, but he felt an overpowering need to be close to the woman he loved.

And he did love her! He hadn't realized how much until he'd thought she had plunged to her death. As he hugged the cliff and edged toward Rissa, who watched him in wide-eyed horror, Drew suddenly realized that all of the situations that he had thought kept Rissa and him apart didn't really amount to anything.

"Lord, if we come out of this," he started to pray, but the ledge beneath his feet crumbled, and he took a flying leap toward the wider bench where Rissa sat. As he landed on his stomach beside her, he thanked God that she hadn't been on that ledge. He crawled to her and gathered her close. His pulse was pounding, and he felt her heartbeat mix with his. God willing, they'd never be separated again. As the beacon plunged the ledge into darkness, he claimed her lips and crushed her to him. He didn't know how much time passed before Mick called, "I'm back."

Drew released Rissa reluctantly.

"I'm on the ledge with Rissa now," he shouted.

"When the beacon passes this way again, I'll drop the rope and the harness. You be ready to catch it."

"I'll send Rissa up first. Do you have anyone with you?"

"Yes, a state cop."

"Then the two of you should be able to lift her."

There was barely room for both of them to stand, but putting his back against one of the spindly evergreens, Drew secured the harness around Rissa's shoulders and waist and assured himself that the hook was fastened securely.

Conscious of her trembling body, he held her snugly and kissed the top of her head. "You'll be all right now. She's ready, Mick."

The rope tightened and slowly Rissa was pulled upward. Her body swayed back and forth, twisted, and occasionally grazed the cliff. Ten minutes later Drew was also lifted to safety, and he hurried to where Rissa lay on the rough ground.

"I've already called 9-1-1," Mick said.

"Are you hurt?" Drew asked, pulling her robe around her shoulders and fastening the buttons.

"My knees hurt where I banged them against the bluffs while they were pulling me up. And I landed on my back when I was thrown over the cliff. It hurts, but I can move, so I must not have broken anything."

"When you were thrown over?" Drew said, his investigative mind suddenly alert. "Who did it?"

"Maybe she shouldn't try to talk," Mick suggested.

The wail of an ambulance approaching rapidly pierced the night air, and Drew said, "When they get here, we won't have a chance to question her." He lifted Rissa slightly, and let her lean against him. "Do you feel like talking?"

"There's not too much to tell. I couldn't sleep and I went downstairs to get something to eat. At the back door, I heard two people talking, and I'm sure they were talking about me. One person…"

"Men or women?" Drew interrupted her.

"I couldn't tell for sure. It may have been a man and a woman. One muttered, 'Are you sure she didn't recognize you?' and the other said, 'I had my mask on and it was dark in the room.' I opened the door, and they must have heard me, for they stopped talking."

"But why didn't you stay in the house or go and notify the guard in the hall?" Drew demanded, irritated because she had risked her life.

"I didn't even think about the cop on duty. I was so scared I couldn't think. I didn't intend to leave the house, but when I went back to my room, I saw someone wearing a black robe leaving the grounds and heading this way. I thought it was our chance to find out who's causing all of our trouble. I must have passed by whomever it was because when I got up here, no one was here."

She swallowed with difficulty and her voice trembled. With a gentle hand, Drew smoothed her wind-blown hair away from her face.

"Then someone slipped up behind me wearing the same kind of mask the person I saw in the library was wearing when my mother was killed. I tried to get away, but I was picked up and pitched over the bluffs."

Mick whistled. "It would have had to be a man to pick you up."

"Or a big woman who knows how to handle people," Drew countered speculatively.

"One last question before the EMTs arrive. Do you have any suspicion at all as to who attacked you?"

She shook her head.

"Rissa, you've got to tell, even if you suspect someone in your family," Drew said sternly. "There's a killer running loose, and we have to find him."

Tears seeped from her eyes. "I don't know who it was."

Drew knew he had to leave it at that.

"One of us will have to notify the family," Mick said.

"You do it. I'm staying with her," Drew said.

Mick gave him a surprised look.

Drew cuffed Mick on the shoulder. "Thanks, partner. I was sure happy to see that homely mug of yours looking over the cliff."

"Anytime, buddy. Anytime!"

"I'll call for a couple of men to search the area, but whoever it was has had plenty of time to get away by now."

"Unless they live in Blanchard Manor," Mick said meaningfully.

"I'll follow the ambulance to the hospital."

It seemed to Drew that it took hours for the EMTs to check Rissa's vitals and lift her onto the gurney. He and Mick took hold of one side of the gurney and helped the other two men carry Rissa downhill to the ambulance that was parked by the paved road with lights flashing. As they prepared to secure Rissa inside, Mick asked her, "Who's in the house tonight?"

"Juliet came this afternoon, so that means three of my sisters are at home, plus Aunt Winnie and Father. And of course Grandfather and his nurse are there, as well as the household staff."

"The same ones there when Trudy was killed...except for Juliet," Drew answered, cringing inwardly with the knowledge that if Rissa hadn't warned him she was going to the bluffs, there would be one less Blanchard now.

"I'll hurry down and rouse the house," Mick said. "I

hope the cop on duty or the one patrolling the grounds saw something."

"Does it occur to you that we're dealing with a cunning killer or somebody who's a mental case?" Drew asked.

"I'll vote for the last possibility. A screw must be loose somewhere."

"And I wonder if we aren't overlooking the possibility of somebody other than the family who's hiding in that house," Drew said.

"Could be! I've heard that the house has enough underground passages, turrets and rooms to hide a small army. A lot of these big mansions along the coast used to be hideouts for smugglers, although I don't know that Blanchard Manor has that kind of history."

Rissa was still being checked out by the E.R. doctor when Portia, Winnie and Ronald rushed into the waiting room where Drew sat. A green-eyed blond girl followed, and Drew assumed she was Juliet.

Portia rushed to Drew, her brown eyes wide with alarm. "What have you learned?

"Nothing official. But as far as I know, she's all right."

"According to Campbell, you know more about this than anybody else," Ronald said, his voice seething with anger.

Drew had been debating how much to tell Rissa's family. "I don't know a whole lot. She called me around ten o'clock and told me that she'd gone downstairs to get something to eat and overheard voices outside the back door. She returned to her room and saw someone leaving the property, wearing the same kind of clothes the person who killed Trudy Blanchard had worn. This unknown person headed up the trail to the bluffs. Rissa decided to follow. I tried to discourage her but she hung up on me. I took off right away, but didn't get there in time."

"Why would she be dumb enough to do that?" Ronald muttered, as if he didn't believe Drew. "Why didn't she tell me? I was just down the hall a few feet away."

Drew wondered what Ronald would say if he suggested that Rissa might have suspected he was the one she was following.

"I don't know," he answered instead.

"Why didn't you tell her to stay in the house?"

"I just told you—I did. But she hung up on me."

"Mick said that Rissa was thrown over the cliff and that you saved her," Winnie said.

"I can't take all the credit, but I helped get her to safety."

Winnie crossed to firmly grasp Drew's hand. "You have my thanks," she said with tears of relief welling in her eyes.

A nurse came into the waiting room. "I need a member of the family to sign some papers. I also need insurance information, as well as a list of medications. Mr. Lancaster didn't have that information."

"I'll sign the papers," Ronald said, and apparently the nurse knew who he was because she didn't question his right to assume responsibility for Rissa.

"I brought her purse," Portia said. She withdrew a small case and handed several cards to the nurse. "She doesn't take any medication, except an aspirin sometimes."

Drew felt sure that if anyone in the family knew that Rissa was taking the antidepressant, it would be Portia. However, Rissa had said that he was the only one who knew that she was being treated for clinical depression. If the medical team didn't know what she was taking, they might give her something that could harm her. Although he was betraying Rissa's confidence, he had to tell them about her medication.

"She *was* taking medicine," he said.

Rissa's family turned to stare at him.

"How do you know?" Ronald demanded.

"She told me. Portia, check her purse—she may have kept it in there."

The purse was large, and Portia sat down and started riffling through the contents. She finally extracted a cosmetic bag, unzipped it and pulled out a small plastic bottle. She read the label aloud.

"Why, that's an antidepressant!" Juliet exclaimed.

"Here's another bottle—the same prescription, filled in Stoneley, the day we met you and Mick for lunch," Portia said. "And the doctor's name is on the label—a well-known woman psychiatrist in New York."

"Why would my daughter need to see a psychiatrist?" Ronald protested.

Although he was concerned about Rissa, Drew stifled his laughter. Living in a zoo like Blanchard Manor could drive anybody up the wall. Portia handed the bottles to the nurse. In the loud, heated discussion of why Rissa was taking an antidepressant and why she hadn't told anyone, Drew slipped unnoticed out of the waiting room, flashed his badge and drifted down the hallway. He hoped for a chance to talk to Rissa before her family was admitted.

THIRTEEN

Rissa believed they must have given her a sedative of some kind because she went to sleep while she was still in the exam room on a bed that felt as hard and cold as a slab of marble. She roused when she was wheeled into a curtained alcove along a long hallway. The nurse covered her with a warm blanket.

"I'll bring your family in now," she said. "The doctor will want to talk to them."

From his vantage point near the E.R. exam room, Drew saw where they took Rissa and he hurried to the room. He had been in E.R. often enough that the nurse recognized him, and she knew he was the one who'd brought Rissa in.

"Delay the others just a few minutes," he said.

This wasn't an unusual request, for often the authorities needed to talk to a victim before the family came in. "I'll give you ten minutes," the nurse agreed.

Drew walked inside the alcove and pulled the curtain. He moved a chair close to Rissa's bed and lifted the hand that didn't have an IV.

"How do you feel?"

"Lousy. How do I look?" she countered with a tired expression in her eyes.

"Beautiful."

Her lips curved into a wan smile. "Did I dream what happened on the ledge or was that real?"

He didn't know if she meant her fall or the moment they had shared before she'd been pulled to safety. "You weren't dreaming," he said. He stood, leaned over and kissed her lips softly. "And you aren't dreaming now."

She took his left hand and held it against her face.

"Your family will be here soon, and I want to talk to you about something else before they come in. The nurse asked about medication and Portia said you didn't take anything, but no one knew that."

"Except you. I didn't want my family to know."

"Well, they know now. I had to tell them."

She gasped and dropped his hand. "Why did you do that?"

"Don't be mad at me, but the hospital staff had to know. If they'd given you something that counteracted with the antidepressant, it could have killed you. I couldn't risk that. Please tell me that you understand."

"It's all right," she said wearily. "I would have told them eventually, but with everything that's been going on the past three months, I didn't want to give them anything else to worry about."

The nurse tapped on the wooden panel beside the curtain. "Time's up, Detective Lancaster."

Drew was standing several feet away from the bed

when the nurse drew back the curtain. Ronald shot a hostile glance toward him as he stalked inside, dominating the small room with his overbearing personality and intimidating stature.

"Why did you do such a stupid thing?" he demanded, advancing angrily toward Rissa. Drew clenched his fists. If the man wasn't so many years older than he was, and Rissa's father, he might have decked the guy. Rissa didn't need a tongue-lashing!

She didn't answer as she was diverted by her sisters and Winnie crowding around her bed. They drew back when the doctor, wearing his green scrubs and cap, stepped inside and spoke to Ronald.

"She's in stable condition. There are no broken bones, but she does have a bad bruise on her left hip." Turning his gaze to Rissa, he said, "You're a very lucky woman."

"I know," she said softly, willing herself not to look at Drew. "But it's more than luck. I was really afraid when I was thrown over the cliff, but when I landed on the ledge, I remembered a Bible verse reminding me that God was watching over me."

Drew felt as if he were in church while he watched the serenity on Rissa's face as she softly quoted, "'If you make the Most High your dwelling—even the Lord, who is my refuge—then no harm will befall you, no disaster will come near your tent. For He will command His angels concerning you to guard you in all your ways; they will lift you up in their hands, so that you will not strike your foot against a stone.'

"I claimed that promise," Rissa whispered, "and then

Drew came. I didn't feel alone after that, for God had sent him to help me."

Drew felt like kneeling right there, at that moment, to pour out his heart to God. God had answered his prayer to save Rissa, so that meant God had never turned his back on him. God had been there all the time—all he needed to do was acknowledge Him and make Jesus Lord of his life. His wandering days were over, and he purposed in his heart that from this day forward, God would be his guide.

"The nurses will take you to a room now," the doctor said.

"For how long?" Rissa asked.

"We'll see," the doctor said evasively.

Portia kissed Rissa as they wheeled her out of the room and started to follow until the doctor indicated by a gesture that he wanted to talk to the family. Drew stepped out in the hall, but stayed within hearing distance.

"I understand from the nurse that none of you were aware that your sister is taking antidepressants."

"That's right," Ronald said. "And I find it hard to believe."

"Believe it," the doctor said. "The prescription is for a mild antidepressant, and the bottle filled by the local pharmacy contains that. The other bottle, although it resembles the prescribed medication in appearance, is a hallucinogen, which in itself might cause problems. But a mixture of the two can cause either auditory or visual hallucinations. Do any of you know if Miss Blanchard has been hallucinating?"

"Of course not," Ronald said. "She's a Blanchard!"

"You didn't know," Winnie told her brother, "but she has had problems since she's been home. She's heard a woman wailing. And she came running to me one day saying that she'd found a threatening note under her pillow. When we went to the room, there was no note, and the bed was made up. She couldn't have seen a note under the pillow if one had been there."

"I don't believe it," Ronald said.

Ignoring him, the doctor said, "Have you noticed any suicidal tendencies?"

"No," Aunt Winnie replied, and the sisters shook their heads. Ronald said nothing.

Drew stepped back into the alcove. "Detective," the doctor said, "you reported that someone threw Miss Blanchard over the bluffs. Did you see that? Or are you going on her word?"

"I didn't see anyone on the bluff when I got there, but I did hear running footsteps through the brush."

"Which could have been a deer or another wild animal," Ronald said.

"No. I recognize human footsteps when I hear them."

The doctor wasn't convinced. "But it's possible that she had a mental lapse and jumped off that cliff. For her own protection, I suggest that Miss Blanchard should be admitted into our psychiatric facility for seventy-two hours. If she's talked to you about her depression more than others, as a police officer, you can make the recommendation."

"Absolutely not!" Drew said. "She's as sane as the

rest of us in this room. If Rissa said that someone threw her off the cliff, that's what happened." He took a deep breath to steady his rattled emotions. "I don't how those hallucinogens got in her purse, but she didn't know what they were when she took them. Somebody has set her up. It would only exacerbate her depression to be. locked up for three days."

"It's my opinion," Ronald said, "that as her father, I should make any decision concerning Rissa. Doctor, if you believe she should be admitted, I'll order it."

The czar of Stoneley has spoken! Drew thought ironically. Who would dare to defy the formidable CEO of Blanchard Fabrics? Drew knew his hands were tied. He didn't have any authority to prevent Rissa from being confined. But he cringed when he remembered that she panicked at the notion of being locked away the way her mother was. The experience of being locked up for three days could easily cause Rissa to lose her sanity. He had to do something to help her.

Rissa woke up alone in a small room. She must have gone to sleep on the way from the E.R. to this room. She had an IV in her arm, so she assumed that she was being given a mild sedative to make her sleep. She felt rested, but when she shifted in bed, she was aware of a sore spot on her hip. Considering what might have happened, she wasn't concerned about a bruise.

Her life during the past few weeks had been one crisis after the other, and being thrown over the cliff was high on her list of traumatic incidents, but she would always remember the experience because of what had happened between her and Drew on the ledge. He had called her *sweetheart,* and the kiss they'd shared proved without a doubt that she loved Drew. And although he hadn't said so, she believed that he loved her, too. Would the dangerous experience they had shared cause Drew to forget his determination not to marry? She didn't know, but right now she was content to think about what had happened between them. God would take care of their future as He had her near death at the hand of an unknown predator.

She assumed that the doctor had only admitted her for observation, and she wished he would come in. She felt well enough to go home now, but she guessed she would have to resign herself to an overnight stay.

Someone fumbled at the door and a lock turned. A nurse eased into the room, closed and locked the door behind her.

"How are we feeling?" she asked and checked the IV.

"A little sore but otherwise I'm all right."

"Your aunt and sisters want to see you. I'll send them in one at a time, but for brief visits only."

Why would her family be hanging around to visit her when she would soon be home?

The nurse exited the room, and Rissa heard a lock turn. Why was she locked in? She surveyed the room. The only window was a long, narrow one near the ceiling. Besides the bed, the only furniture was one straight chair. The walls were bare and Rissa felt suffocated. A door to the right led into a bathroom. She couldn't stay here. She swung her feet over the side of the bed, but was restrained by the IV tube in her arm.

The door opened and Aunt Winnie walked in. "How are you, dear one?"

"Aunt Winnie! Why am I locked in this room?"

Winnie patted her on the shoulder. "Now, don't get upset. This is just a precautionary measure. Taking two different kinds of medicine may have caused you to hallucinate."

"I have not been taking two medications. I didn't imagine hearing people talking about me. I did not imagine that someone threw me over that cliff."

"Yes, dear," Winnie soothed. "Try to relax. As soon as the doctor gets your medication regulated you can be released. You should have told us that you were having problems."

"It wasn't that important—no need to worry the rest of you."

One by one Portia and Juliet came to see her, as well as Peg Henderson. Rissa wanted to scream, for they all obviously thought she had tried to commit suicide. But she suffered in silence, for she didn't want to give them any other reason to think she was insane.

"I feel like one of the family," Peg said, "and I was concerned about you. I must hurry back though."

When the housekeeper came in next, Rissa wondered who was looking after Grandfather, but she did appreciate their concern. All of the visits were brief, and since she dozed most of the rest of the day, she supposed that they were keeping her medicated.

She didn't have on any clothes except the hospital gown and they'd taken away her watch. There wasn't any clock on the wall, so she had no way of reckoning time. The hours seemed to pass slowly as she drifted in and out of slumber.

She stirred when someone touched her shoulder and shook her gently.

"Rissa, wake up."

Drew's voice! Her eyes popped open.

"What are you doing here?"

He held his fingers to his lips to silence her. "I'm releasing you from the hospital." He dropped a plastic bag on the bed and started disconnecting the IV from her arm. "Your clothes are in there. Hurry and change. We don't have much time."

"Are you taking me home?"

"No, your father would just commit you again. I've arranged for you to stay a few days at Hideaway, a safe house."

"Should you be doing this?"

"No, but I've already broken in, so what else I do won't make any difference. Hurry!"

He turned his back while she slipped out of the nightgown and put on the sweats. She left the robe in the bag. When she sat on the chair to put on her shoes, Drew knelt before her and tied them for her and helped her stand.

"Ready?" he said.

"Yes. What time is it?"

"Four o'clock in the morning. I figured this was the

best time to get you out. Nobody's stirring much. Keep right behind me."

He opened the door quietly and, holding to his coattail, Rissa followed him down the hall.

"We'll take the stairs instead of the elevator," he said.

Rissa had been housed on the fifth floor and because Drew was rushing her, she was breathless when they reached ground level. When they came to an outside door, Rissa braced for the fire alarm to go off when Drew pushed on the door, but she heard nothing. He looked from right to left before he took her hand, guided her through the door and gingerly pushed the door shut.

Rissa breathed in the fresh air as they ran side by side down the alley to Thornwood Lane where Drew's pickup was parked. He helped her into the cab, slid in beside her, started the motor and eased away from the curb as nonchalantly as if they were going for a joyride.

"Won't you get into a lot of trouble doing this?"

"I've been in trouble before, but it doesn't matter. You'd told me how afraid you are of being locked in and I couldn't leave you there. I figured by the end of three days you *would* be out of your mind. I was determined that wasn't going to happen to you. I made up my mind to get you out if I possibly could."

"I can't imagine how you could get into a locked room and out of that hospital at night without alarms sounding all over the place."

"You're just as well off not to know, but I'll tell you this much. There's an employee at the hospital who owes me a big favor. I had fifteen minutes to get you out. Your family won't be able to take you out of the safe house."

"I can't believe you risked your career for me."

"Good cops are always in demand. And I've told you—I don't intend to stay in Stoneley the rest of my life anyway."

Daylight had come by the time they pulled into the parking lot behind the safe house. Drew exhaled deeply. A few more steps and he'd have Rissa to safety.

"They're expecting us. Bring your things."

He opened the door for her, and she stepped out. A man approached from the side of the building. At first Drew thought he was a staff member coming to help them, but instinctively, he had a hunch that something was wrong. Suddenly a gun appeared in the man's right hand, aimed at Rissa.

Pushing Rissa behind the truck, Drew threw himself toward the man and tackled him around the legs just as the gun exploded. Drew felt a red-hot streak along his left arm, and he knew the bullet had struck him. The man pulled away from Drew and started to run. Throwing his cell phone toward Rissa, Drew shouted, "Call Mick. Reinforcements."

Drew tackled the attacker before he got to the street. The man was strong and as determined to get away as Drew was to restrain him. Rissa's fingers were trembling so much she wasted precious moments holding the phone steady enough to find Mick's number on the listing and to push the button. While the phone rang, she kept her eyes on Drew and the hitman.

God, let him answer. Let him answer.

"Campbell here."

"This is Rissa. Drew and I are in the parking lot of the safe house. Someone tried to shoot us. Drew has him down, but I don't know how long he can hold him."

Mick disconnected, and Rissa laid the phone on the hood of Drew's truck and ran toward the struggling men. As she passed the bed of the truck, she saw a piece of lumber about two feet long. She snatched it up without an idea of how she could use it.

The stranger was smaller than Drew, but he was fighting frantically, intent on escaping. Rissa hefted the wood, moved in close to the fighters and whacked the hitman on the head. His struggling ceased immediately and he collapsed under Drew's body.

Panting, Drew said, "Get handcuffs out of the truck's glove compartment."

"Did I kill him?" she fretted.

"Who cares? Hurry."

She found the handcuffs and gave them to Drew. Blood oozed from the wound on his arm, and Rissa brought a cloth from the pickup and wiped the blood from the wound. When he had restrained the man, Drew looked at his arm.

"It's only a surface wound, so it isn't serious."

"But it should be bandaged."

"There's a first-aid kit in the truck with some gauze in it. Bring it, please."

Too worried about Drew to consider that someone had tried to kill them, she brought the kit to him. Following his instructions, she unwound a large piece of the gauze and wrapped it around his arm.

By the time Mick arrived, the attacker had regained consciousness. As Mick and another cop crowded around them, Drew pulled the stranger to his feet.

"Why did you start shooting at us?" he demanded.

"Man, I was just passing through town," the man protested. "I stopped here expecting to get a handout and you jumped me."

"You shot first."

"I was just pointing the gun to protect myself—trying to scare you off. The gun went off accidentally."

Mick said to the other cop, "Take him into headquarters and lock him up. I don't want him getting away until we question him further."

"Hey," the man protested. "You've got no call to arrest me."

"We will have when Miss Blanchard files a complaint that you fired at her," Drew warned him. "What do you know about the Blanchards?"

"I told you—I'm just passing through town. I ain't acquainted with nobody here."

After the cruiser pulled away, leaving Rissa and Drew alone with Mick, he turned on Drew. "And just what do *you* think you're doing? What's Rissa doing here with you?"

"She checked out of the hospital early this morning, and I was bringing her here for safety."

"Uh-huh! I suppose she's been checked out right and proper."

Drew snapped his fingers. "We just happened to forget to pass by the front desk."

"I've got to report this to the hospital before the whole Blanchard family is stirred up again. If someone calls and tells them that Rissa has disappeared, Ronald will demand that they call out the national guard."

"She's still going to stay here until her seventy-two hours are up," Drew said. "I couldn't leave her in that psych ward when I knew she was afraid of being locked up. Did you know about that?"

"Not until last night when Portia was worrying about it. You know what this could mean, don't you?"

"Yes, she can be forced back into that ward if they catch her—that's why I brought her here."

"I wasn't referring to Rissa. Don't you know how this will affect your career?"

"I do. Don't think I didn't weigh the consequences before I set out last night. When I had to choose between my job and Rissa's welfare, she came first. What would you have done if it had been Portia instead of Rissa?"

Looking from one to the other, Mick said, "So, it's like that, huh?"

Drew put his arm around Rissa. "It's like that."

"Then you have my best wishes." As he turned away, Drew heard him mutter, "You're going to need them."

FOURTEEN

If her father tried to get her removed from Hideaway, Rissa wasn't aware of it, for she spent the next three days assessing the changes the accident had made in her life.

The staff members of the safe house were kind to her, offering any help she needed, but they didn't force her to do anything she didn't want to do. She spent most of the time alone, but she chose to eat her meals with the other residents, which opened up a new world to her.

Never before had she sat at the table with an abused wife and mother, whose husband had broken her arm during a drunken brawl. He had a history of abuse, but the authorities had done nothing to him until he'd killed one of his two sons and physically injured his wife.

Nor had Rissa had any contact with a teenage girl who was trying to shake a drug habit and had no other place to live. And she had never talked with a man who had been wrongfully accused of robbing a bank. Although he'd been proven innocent, he had lost his job and was now penniless because all of his savings had been used for legal fees.

Rissa was convinced that this sojourn at Hideaway had changed her outlook on life forever. When she compared her life to these people, she realized that regardless of her family's quirky behavior, she hadn't been mistreated. She'd never gone to bed hungry, she'd never been penniless and she had never been physically abused.

As she associated with the other residents, her creative juices started flowing, and she suddenly had an idea for her next play. Would the public accept a stage show based around the residents of a safe house? She thought it would, and she was eager to run the idea past her agent. When she'd been agonizing over it for several weeks, who would have thought that the terrible experience she'd had would lead to the subject of her next play? More than ever in her life, Rissa was confident of the truth of the psalmist's words *In all your ways acknowledge Him and He will direct your path.*

But more than anything else, the quiet retreat provided ample time to reflect on her relationship with Drew, which had definitely taken a positive turn. Could they possibly make a happy marriage? He was small-town; she was city. He didn't have a college education; she had graduated from Yale. Drew came from a poor, uncultured family; for centuries, her family's roots had dipped deeply into Maine's highest social and cultural background.

Stop it! she scolded herself. *You'll never build a relationship with negative thoughts. Consider what you have in common.*

They both loved the Lord, and that was an adequate

foundation for any marriage. Even though Drew admitted that he'd strayed away from the Christian teaching of his childhood, in the few days she'd known him, she'd definitely seen his thoughts turning toward God.

They had both been scarred by incidents in their childhood. His father had been abusive and had abandoned him, and her father had never shown any affection for his daughters. In fact, after this episode, Rissa had the feeling that her father would disown her, which would place her and Drew on the same level.

Both of them were eager to sacrifice to reach goals they'd set for themselves. They enjoyed the other's company. When they were together, she never considered that she and Drew were of a different class. By the end of her tenure at Hideaway, Rissa knew that she loved Drew. Based on love and their Christian faith, she believed they could make a life.

When Drew came to pick Rissa up, he wore a pair of jeans and a plaid flannel shirt. He didn't have on a badge or a revolver. She had been worried that Drew might have been fired because he had helped her escape from the hospital, and the absence of his uniform made her concerned that had happened. Of course, it might be that he just wasn't on duty now.

"You look great," he said as they drove away from the safe house.

"And I feel rested and ready to take on the world again. I've come to the conclusion that my depression has stemmed from the pressure of last-minute preparations for the opening of my show. Coupled with all the problems we've had at Stoneley since the first of the year, I had more than anyone could bear."

"I don't want to upset your newfound euphoria, but you can't forget that somebody tried to kill you, so you have to be cautious. In fact, two people have made attempts on your life—I'm sure that hitman was after you. So you're a threat to somebody."

"But I don't know *anything!*" she protested.

"Whoever is responsible for the murder of your mother doesn't know that. I wish you would go back to New York and stay there until this crime wave at Stoneley is over. I'll miss seeing you, but I want you to be safe. And you aren't safe at Blanchard Manor."

"I won't leave until after my mother's funeral, but I will go then if the police release me. I noticed the absence of your cop regalia. What's happened?"

"I've been suspended from duty without pay for a month. It may be an indefinite suspension after that."

"And it's all my fault."

"Don't flatter yourself," he said, but his warm smile took the sting out of his words. "I knew what I was doing."

"You don't seem much concerned about it."

"I think the chief is on my side and certainly most of the department is rooting for me, but he had no choice except to suspend me. I broke the law, and I need to be chastised. But I'd do it again in a heartbeat. To see you looking as serene as you do today has paid me in full for any problems I have."

Drew drove slowly, not at the breakneck pace he usually traveled, and Rissa told him about her experiences in the safe house and her plans for the future based on that.

"I needed some time away from everyone to sort out my future. I've never felt closer to God than during the time I was cut off from the rest of the world. He's given me direction for the future."

"Does that future include me?"

"Probably—if you want it that way," she said, and there was a gentleness in her voice.

"And I do. Although I'm not sure how I'll fit in your life."

Rissa placed her fingers over his lips. "Don't even think it! That's one of the things the enforced solitude brought to my attention. We need to focus on the positive. I did and was amazed at how much we're alike."

"God has been directing my thoughts along the same line. The past several days, we've worked together as a team. I've helped you—you've helped me. I would never have subdued that hitman if you hadn't banged him on the head."

"What did you find out about him?"

"Not much. They booked him by the name of Conrad Keefer, which turned out to be an alias. He still sticks to his story that he was only passing through Stoneley. He says he had never heard of the Blanchards, but that he saw my uniform and thought I was going to kill him. He's spent more time in jail than out for the past ten years. He'll be taken back to the state prison in a few days, for he's broken his parole by carrying a firearm."

"And you still think he was trying to kill me?"

"Yes. I'm not exactly a novice in law enforcement, and I know he wasn't pointing the gun at me, but at you. Whoever threw you over that cliff sent that man to kill you. I'm convinced of it."

"But how could he have known where to find me?"

"That's been puzzling me, too. Nobody knew except me. I'd made arrangements to bring you to the safe house, but I hadn't told anyone. I didn't even tell my accomplice in the hospital what I intended to do. I just persuaded him to play blind for a short time."

"I suppose the gunman could have followed us to the safe house."

"Maybe, but I didn't waste any time. If he followed us, he couldn't have gotten there before we did. Somehow that man learned where I was taking you and got there before we did."

"Maybe he was hiding in the hallway and overheard what you said to me."

"That's as good an explanation as I can imagine. I only know that someone means harm to you, and I can't seem to protect you. I wish you could have stayed at the safe house until after your mother's funeral. I'm worried about you, and I can't watch you all the time."

"I know this sounds strange, because I was so fearful before, but because God has protected me through several incidents, I don't believe He will let anything happen to me."

Drew's eyes were gentle and contemplative. "You may be right."

"I'm convinced of it. In the past few days, I've been

delivered from death twice. I read a lot of Psalms while I was in the safe house, and I kept coming back to a psalm written by David when he was being pursued by his enemies. He praised God's deliverance by saying 'They spread a net for my feet—I was bowed down in distress. They dug a pit in my path—but they have fallen into it themselves.' I'm confident that the mystery is going to be solved without any further harm coming to me."

"I pray that's true, and I believe it is, but I still can't help but worry that something will destroy our happiness. I'm not very good at this proposing business—I've had no practice at it. What I started to say was that we do have a lot going for us. I want to marry you, Rissa. If you feel the same way, we'll work out the why and wherefores later."

Her heart swelled. "I want to marry you," she murmured tenderly.

He stopped the car, pulled to the side of the road. His hands slipped up her arms and brought her closer.

"This is pretty public, isn't it?"

Laughing into her hair, he said, "Who cares? I'd just as soon shout it from the housetops, but I suppose we'll have to wait a little longer."

She settled against him, savoring the feel of his arms around her. She had never felt so secure in her life. Burying her face in his neck, she breathed a caress there. When she lifted her face to him, Drew's kiss touched her like a whisper.

Sighing, he released her and scooted behind the wheel. "I can't help wondering if *I'm* hallucinating or dreaming," he murmured. "But my dreams have never been as pleasant as this."

"Are you going to ask Father, or will we just tell him?"

"Knowing what I do about him, I'm sure he will never give his blessing on a marriage between us. As far as I'm concerned, I'd just as soon tell him after we're married."

"Maybe we could have a double wedding with Mick and Portia."

"We can't decide on a date until I'm sure I have a job. The last two days I've been preparing a résumé to be sent to police departments in the New York City area and also to neighboring New Jersey. I won't send it until I know what the outcome of my suspension is."

"I'm sure you can get a job there."

"You know my interest in airplanes. I'd like to connect to a department where they have helicopter patrols. I've thought that my dreams to fly would never happen, but after I've met you, I'm ready to reach for the stars."

"My goal is to become successful in the city's show business. So we'll reach for the stars together."

"Suits me. I'll gladly enter your world."

"Maybe diversity is a good thing in a marriage. I'll enjoy introducing you to my life."

Blanchard Manor came in sight and Rissa was amazed at how little the stern facade intimidated her today. Would marriage to Drew finally break the hold that had tied her to the past?

"I'm going in to help you face the music, but now that I'm no longer on the force, there will be other officers watching the family. You can call me when you have an opportunity."

"I may leave with you," Rissa said, and the thought didn't bother her at all. "I wouldn't be at all surprised if Father forbids me to enter the house."

Laughing, he opened the car door for her. "That doesn't seem to bother you."

She squeezed his hand. "Thanks to you—nothing bothers me today."

Apparently no one was aware of their arrival, for the door didn't open. Rissa punched in the code and walked before Drew into the hallway. An officer waved to them from his chair next to the stair steps.

"Aunt Winnie," Rissa called.

Her aunt came to the top of the stairs, and Portia and Juliet rushed out of the living room. Whatever the others thought, these three were glad to see her. They gathered around Rissa to welcome her home.

"We've been so worried about you," Portia said. "Do you really think someone tried to kill you?"

Drew turned toward the door, and Winnie said, "Mr. Lancaster, thanks for bringing Rissa home."

"My pleasure," he said and left the house without a backward look.

Portia put her arm around Rissa and drew her into the living room. "We want to hear about everything that happened to you."

"Why didn't you tell us you were being treated for depression?" Aunt Winnie asked.

"Because it was just a mild case and there was no

reason to worry you. I have no idea how those hallucinogens got in that bottle, but it had to be done by someone who wanted to make me think I was crazy. I've never taken anything except what the doctor prescribed."

"So you did hear a woman wailing?"

"I'm sure I did, but why I would be the only one in the family to hear that, I don't know. I didn't imagine that note, either. And because nobody except Drew believed me, I didn't tell you that someone had also put a picture of you and me, Portia, and our mother in my dresser drawer."

"Is someone in this house responsible for all that's happening?" Juliet asked. "It scares me just to think about it."

"I'm not convinced that it's anybody who lives in the house. As smart as this person seems to be, they would be crafty enough to disable our security system and get in the house without us knowing it."

"Do you think the person who threw you over the cliff was the same person you saw in the library?" Portia asked.

"Whoever it was wore a similar mask and dark robe. That's all I know."

Miranda and Bianca came into the room, and Rissa stood to give Bianca a hug. She had always admired her because she had defied her father's wishes and had attended law school and become a successful lawyer. Observing her performance in the courtroom, no one would suspect that Bianca was the shyest of all the sisters, but since her romance with Leo Santiago, an executive at Blanchard Fabrics, Bianca had blossomed from the happiness she had found with him.

"Sit down," Aunt Winnie said. "Rissa is ready to tell us what's happened."

Rissa settled on a settee beside her aunt, while the sisters gathered close. Juliet and Portia sat on the floor, but Miranda and Bianca took their places on the other settee.

Starting with her trip downstairs for a midnight snack, she told them about the people she'd heard conspiring, and her sudden decision to follow the person leaving Blanchard Manor and going into the woods.

Shuddering, Portia said angrily, "Why didn't you wake me so I could go with you? To think I slept through all of that!"

"I acted in haste, without thinking, I'll admit."

"Stop interrupting," Miranda said, "and let her finish."

Rissa told them about the harrowing experience that had almost taken her life, not once but twice. Her tone must have softened when she spoke of Drew, for Miranda and Bianca exchanged skeptical glances. Portia giggled, and Rissa's face flushed when Juliet said, "Don't tell me we're going to have another detective in this family!"

She was saved from more razzing from her family when the front door opened and Ronald entered the foyer. He started down the hall to his office, but paused when he saw his family assembled in the living room. His roving eyes settled on Rissa.

"So, you've finally come home! I wonder how you had the nerve to darken these doors with your presence when you've added another reason for this community to ridicule the Blanchards."

"Would you have preferred that I let someone kill me or lose my mind in that psych ward? But I'm ready to go home—I can leave today if you want that."

"I doubt that Rissa's experience can make the gossip any worse than it is already," Juliet said, quick to champion Rissa as well as cast a barb at her father.

"At least the local authorities knew enough to bust Drew Lancaster for his role in your escape," Ronald said in a pleased tone. "That will be the last time he'll play cop and robbers."

Rissa clamped her lips tight to avoid a retort.

"But I will say that I was pleased with his effort to save your life." His lips trembled slightly. "I wouldn't want to lose any of my daughters." He cleared his throat and looked down. Apparently embarrassed at his display of sentiment, he abruptly changed the subject.

"I've just come from the funeral home. Your mother's body is ready for viewing. We'll go at six o'clock as a group to a private viewing. The funeral home will not open to the public until after we've been there. The casket will be closed during the funeral tomorrow." He surveyed the room. "Hasn't Delia gotten here yet?"

"She called from New York. She'll arrive this afternoon."

The experience of seeing her mother in the casket would remain in her memory as one of the worst moments of Rissa's life. The eight family members were taken in the limousine to the back door of the funeral home, where they were admitted by the funeral director. They followed him in a deathly silence down a hallway—Ronald and Winnie leading the way, and the six sisters in birth order behind them.

Organ music played softly as they entered a small room. Portia and Rissa clasped hands as they waited their turn to file by the casket. An arrangement of Easter lilies and greenery was draped over a nearby table. Ronald had carried the ostentation even to the floral display—the arrangement would cover the entire casket.

He smoothed Trudy's hair, rearranged a diamond necklace—a Blanchard heirloom—lying on the white silk dress that had been ordered from a boutique in Boston. He bent and kissed her cheek.

Standing behind the twins, Juliet muttered in disgust. "How can he be such a hypocrite?" she whispered in Rissa's ear.

Aunt Winnie laid her hand on the handcrafted wooden casket and seemed genuinely sorrowful to see the face of the woman whom she had considered a sister and a friend. Miranda and Bianca, the only ones who could remember their mother and had mourned her death all of their lives, wound their arms around each other and sobbed. Rissa didn't know Portia's sentiments, but she felt nothing. If it hadn't been for Trudy's marked resemblance to Juliet, she could have been looking at a stranger.

Delia paused only momentarily before she walked to a chair and sat down.

Juliet had walked alone into the funeral home, and Portia and Rissa stood on each side of their youngest sister as she looked at her mother. Juliet had always blamed herself for their mother's death, because until they'd learned that their mother had still been alive, the sisters had all thought their mother's death had been indirectly caused by the postpartum depression resulting from Juliet's birth.

Rissa couldn't comprehend how her youngest sister must feel, so she put her arm around Juliet's waist and squeezed tightly. That was all she could do, but it seemed to be enough, for when they walked away from the casket, Juliet kissed Rissa's cheek.

Although she had slept well at the safe house the night before, in spite of her feeling that all was at peace in her heart, Rissa slept very little that night. Her whole being seemed poised, as if she waited for the funeral so she could put this death behind her and return to her life in New York. But how could she leave when so many issues were still unresolved?

Why had Trudy Blanchard come to the library on the night she'd been killed?

Who had murdered her and why?

Had the hitman been after Drew or was she the intended victim?

If someone was determined to kill her, would that person follow her to the city?

Was some member of her immediate family responsible for these crimes?

With her mind in such turmoil, Rissa finally gave up on sleep and sat in a chair until daylight.

FIFTEEN

The funeral was scheduled for eleven o'clock. Again the Blanchard family appeared to be unified as they traveled by limousine to the church. Ronald had given the servants time off to attend the funeral, leaving only Howard and Peg at home.

Rissa hadn't expected many people to attend, and she was astounded at the masses standing outside the church waiting to be admitted. Since most of them had never even known Trudy, they couldn't have been there to mourn her. And because Ronald was such a pain in the neck to most people, very few would have come to empathize with him. Undoubtedly the crowd had gathered out of curiosity.

But she wondered how much their curiosity would be satisfied. Because very few could watch the family during the memorial service, no one would know how grief-stricken they were. Except for the impressive spray of flowers on the casket, no flowers were on display, so they wouldn't find out how many floral offerings had been received.

Although the church would accommodate a congregation of two hundred, Rissa estimated from the size of the throng that not everyone could be seated. Drew stood beside the curb when the limousine arrived, and he and Rissa exchanged significant glances. She was comforted to know that he was near her.

The church remained locked until the Blanchard family arrived and took their places in an alcove that separated them from the other mourners. Soft music welled from the pipe organ as the family was seated, and Rissa listened to the subdued murmuring as the congregation gathered inside the sanctuary. Aunt Winnie must have had a hand in choosing the musical pieces because selections from Bach, Mozart and Haydn as well as familiar hymns were played.

As she waited for the memorial service to begin, Rissa enjoyed being once again in the church where her spiritual values were nurtured. Unity Christian Church had been a landmark in Stoneley for many years. The building's tall spire, capped by a cupola and a weather cock, contained a bell cast by Paul Revere and Son in 1803, which still summoned the congregation to worship each Lord's Day. An extensive renovation fifty years ago had altered the exterior of the church from its former clapboard appearance to a brick-faced edifice. But the original sanctuary had been preserved in its simple but attractive dignity.

The building was five windows wide with the upper windows tucked tightly under the narrow eaves. The tall, prominently placed wooden pulpit and sounding board were located in the center of the long wall opposite the entrance. Each pew faced the pulpit, as did the galleries that projected from the other three walls. Massive roof timbers and a plastered ceiling hovered over the sanctuary.

Enclosed stairways provided access to the galleries. The Blanchard family sat in a curtained area under the gallery to the left of the pulpit where they were secluded from the curious eyes of most of the congregation.

Before the service began, Tate Connolly, Aunt Winnie's youthful sweetheart, who had just recently re-entered her life, incited Ronald's anger by entering the family section to take an empty chair beside Winnie. Rissa smiled and nudged Portia with her elbow. She thought it was cute that Aunt Winnie had a beau.

But according to Portia, who had gotten the information from Mick, even Tate Connolly was a suspect in the criminal activities that surrounded the Blanchard family. There had been bad blood between the Blanchard and Connolly clans for generations. According to rumor, Howard Blanchard and Lester Connolly, Tate's father, had both loved the same woman. She had chosen Lester, and in revenge Howard had destroyed the Connolly family financially by sabotaging their textile business and seizing the company for himself. Was there no limit to what the men in her family had done? Rissa thought. She shook her head and switched her thoughts back to the memorial service, wondering if her father would create a scene here.

When the family had discussed the funeral, Ronald

had mentioned his plan to deliver a eulogy to his wife, but hadn't persisted when his daughters had vetoed his suggestion. But Rissa wouldn't have been surprised if after he had gotten all of them inside the church, he would take charge as he always did. Or would he dare to alienate Alannah Stafford, who without doubt would be in the crowd? At least they had been spared the humiliation of having the woman seated with the family.

Rissa breathed easier when the minister, Gregory Brown, approached the pulpit, for she didn't believe her father would interrupt him to speak. She didn't know Reverend Brown well, having seen him only a few times, because he had come to Unity Christian Church after she'd gone away to school.

But she was impressed with his kind voice and expression and his handsome features as much as his brief message. He chose to read from the fourteenth chapter of John.

Let not your heart be troubled: you believe in God, believe also in me. In my Father's house are many mansions: if it were not so, I would have told you. I go to prepare a place for you. I will come again, and receive you unto myself; that where I am, there you may be also.

As the minister's soft voice commented on the words he had read, Rissa's heart was calmed. Reverend Brown didn't use the words of Jesus to suggest that the departed would live in earthly mansions in Heaven. That suited Rissa. Living in the Blanchard mansion hadn't brought contentment to any of them. The consensus of the minister's message in simplistic terms seemed to be that Jesus was telling His followers that the splendor of life with God throughout eternity would be superior to any scenario that the earth-ridden mind could conceive.

Rissa prayed that the peace she had experienced through the short service had also found its way into the hearts of her family members. Even as much as she resented her father, she wanted him to find rest for his troubled heart and mind.

Representing the Blanchard family, Ronald and Aunt Winnie stood at the exit to shake hands with those who had attended and to accept their condolences. Juliet silently observed Ronald's solemn countenance, and Rissa should have been warned by her sister's expression to expect the worst.

Only the Blanchard limousine and representatives from the funeral home wound their way to the private cemetery adjacent to the town graveyard. At one time the Blanchard graves had been a part of the community cemetery, but when an ancestor had decided that the Blanchards deserved a private burial place, a fence had been erected around the family plot.

The granite mausoleum was impressive—larger and more ornate than any other crypt in the community— and Rissa knew that her father had planned it that way. But she was past caring about the things her father did. She wanted to put this funeral behind her and move on with her life. She looked toward the future with Drew.

Because the kitchen staff had gone to the funeral, dinner was scheduled to be served later than usual. Rissa had been watching Juliet during the ride home, contemplating the determined expression on her sister's face. Juliet was the first to enter the house, and when the rest were grouped in the hallway removing their coats, Juliet stepped up on the bottom stair step.

"I've got something to say, and I want all of you to step inside the living room."

Ronald lifted his eyebrows. "And when did you start giving the orders around here?"

"Right now!"

Ronald's mouth took on an unpleasant twist, but he bowed ironically and waved his family into the room before him.

Juliet was the last to enter the room and she stood in front of the fireplace. She motioned for everyone to be seated.

"You'd better be sitting down when you hear what I have to say."

Sharing a glance with Portia, Rissa could tell that her twin was as surprised as she was. Rissa stroked her right cheek with the thumb and pinkie finger of her left hand, signaling that she had no idea what Juliet was up to. Portia nodded in agreement.

The six women sat on the twin settees. Ronald stood ramrod straight beside the door.

Looping her thumbs into the belt of her long silk skirt, Juliet looked pointedly at her father. Pulling a deep breath, she said, "Do you know Arthur Sinclair?"

Ronald's face turned a pasty white, and he didn't answer.

"I've been sitting on this particular bit of news for

several weeks," Juliet said, her green eyes snapping in anger. "I wasn't sure that I would ever tell anyone what I've learned." Staring directly at Ronald, she said, "But after your pious show of devotion and love today, I can't remain quiet any longer."

The fringe of Juliet's lashes cast shadows on her cheeks as she purposely scanned the faces of her sisters and aunt. "Ronald Blanchard is not my father. Arthur Sinclair is."

A quick intake of breath escaped Ronald's lips, and he stared at Juliet, quick anger rising in his eyes.

"While you were vacationing all over Europe with Alannah Stafford," she said to Ronald, "I've been running down information to learn about my true paternity. I had to go as far as California before I learned the truth." She turned to face her sisters. "Ronald Blanchard, the man I've always thought was my father and could never understand why he hated me, is not my father. Our mother had an affair with Arthur Sinclair, who is now a tenured professor at the University of California. I'm the result of that affair."

"Oh, no," Miranda cried out and laid her head on the arm of the settee.

"It's true. When I tracked him down, he admitted to the affair. I was prepared to hate the man, but when I learned that he had just recently learned that he was my father, I forgave him."

"But how would he have learned that?" Winnie said.

"Because our mother contacted him after she escaped from the mental institution and asked him for money to start a new life. My father said that Mother wouldn't give him any details except that she feared for her daughters, especially me, if my true paternity was made known. He gave her some money, but he had no idea where she went after that."

"Could the fact that you knew that information have caused the attempt on your life last month?" Bianca asked.

"I'm sure it did," Juliet said, and her eyes sparkled angrily. She turned to face Ronald.

"You might be able to pull the wool over the eyes of others, but you aren't fooling me at all. If you didn't kill our mother here in the library, at least I feel sure that you're indirectly responsible for her death."

"That's a lie," Ronald shouted in his own defense. "I resented her affair as any man would, and I had never forgiven her. But when I saw her lying dead on the library floor, I realized that I'd never stopped loving her. That's the reason her affair had hurt me so much." His voice cracked. "And contrary to what you think, Juliet, I never hated you. I cherish you as if you were my own."

"If that's your way of *cherishing* someone, then I want no part of it," Juliet said bitterly. "And I don't believe that you loved my mother, either."

"Well, you're wrong. Ever since Trudy was killed, I've been reliving the years of happiness we had." Almost pleading, Ronald looked from one woman to the other. "Don't you see? I loved her, and I'm heartbroken because we missed so many years together. Can't you understand that?"

His earnest gaze moved from his sister to each of his

daughters. When he apparently found no sign in their eyes that they believed him, with drooping shoulders he left the room. His retreat down the hallway sounded like the steps of an aged, weary man.

Although Rissa didn't believe that her father still loved Trudy, she did feel sorry for him. A proud man like Ronald would be devastated to have his wife betray him. And it was obvious now why he had always shunned Juliet. When Juliet had grown up to look so much like his wife, every time he'd looked at her he must have been reminded of his wife's unfaithfulness.

Darkness settled once again around Blanchard Manor. In a vacant turret in the rear of the house, a black-robed figure sorted through a box that held various kinds of drugs. How easy it had been to sneak in the poison under the eyes of those who thought they were such good detectives. Holding up a bottle to read the label in a dim light, the individual giggled with delight. Potassium! Just what was needed to right an almost-forgotten wrong!

Slowly the masked person eased down the narrow steps from the turret, unlocked a door with a skeleton key from a ring that held keys affording access to any room in Blanchard Manor. Soundlessly, the apartment door opened.

All was quiet in the room as a sterile hand dropped a potassium tablet and some sugar into Howard's teacup.

Rissa awakened the next morning surprised to hear the sound of hurricane-force winds beating against her window. The weather the day before had been hot for April in Maine, and Sonya, who was gloomy most of the time, anyway, had muttered, "It's a bad sign. Nothing but an omen of bad weather when we have a hot day like that in April."

The room was semidark and Rissa snuggled under the blanket reflecting on Drew and their future. She should have been making preparations to go home, but as much as she missed the city, she knew she would miss Drew more. Thoughts of him had infiltrated her dreams and her waking hours for several weeks before she'd come to Maine. What would it be like now to know that he loved her and to be separated by a few hundred miles? She was convinced that the city wouldn't be as important to her now as it had been a month ago. So that was what love did to you, she thought with a hint of wonder.

Another blast of wind rattled the windows and Portia sat up in bed, stretched and yawned. "What's going on?"

"We're having a storm."

Portia peered at the clock on her nightstand and slid back under the covers. "We don't have to get up for a half hour. Gee, it's cold in here."

"I'll get up and turn on the heat. After yesterday, I'd hoped that spring was here, but it doesn't sound like it."

After she adjusted the thermostat on the gas logs, Rissa wiped steam off the window.

"Portia, it's snowing."

"No wonder I'm cold," her sister muttered, covering her head.

The wet snow had plastered the outside of the

window, and an inch or more of the white stuff was already on the ground. "It must be a full-fledged blizzard," Rissa said. "I can't even see the trees at the edge of the lawn."

"And I was planning to spend the day with Mick and Kaitlyn," Portia groaned.

Still watching the storm, Rissa marveled at Portia's love for Mick's young daughter. When they'd been children, Portia and Rissa had always been delighted when they'd found out that they possessed a habit or preference that the other twin didn't. Portia's utter devotion to children and Rissa's lack of maternal tendencies was one of the most obvious differences that had surfaced lately.

By the time the family gathered for breakfast, the whole estate was blanketed in several inches of snow.

"I won't be going to work today," Ronald said, and Rissa knew he would be like a caged lion. "The storm is expected to blow itself out by mid afternoon but not before it dumps six more inches on us."

"I'm worried about the power going off," Winnie said. "It's a wet, heavy snow, just the kind that hangs on the evergreens and then drops on the electric lines."

"Always borrowing trouble, aren't you?" Ronald said, but his tone wasn't as sarcastic as usual. "But you may be right, so all of us had better prepare for a possible outage."

Winnie put the household staff and her nieces to work. Water would be available and food could be prepared, for Andre preferred a gas stove rather than electric. Most of the fireplace grates had been replaced by gas logs, but in a power outage, the thermostats wouldn't work and it was hard to heat a house as large as theirs. Winnie suggested that everyone should have extra blankets in their room.

By mid afternoon the snow lessened, and a few shafts of sunlight turned the countryside into a winter wonderland. Apparently the cop on guard at the gate had been recalled before the blizzard had struck for there wasn't a cruiser in sight. Blanchard Manor was one of the first places to be plowed out after a blizzard and the snowplow came before the snow had stopped entirely.

"Let's go play in the snow," Rissa said with youthful excitement. After the hardship they'd all endured recently, romping outdoors seemed like the perfect escape. Juliet and Portia readily agreed, and the sisters hurried to find their outdoor clothing.

Drew followed the snowplow to the manor, and he laughed when he saw the twins and Juliet dressed in heavy clothes making a snowman on the lawn. They cheered when they saw him, and he was dazzled by the change in their expressions. He was thankful that the blizzard had provided them with a reason to have some fun. He pulled on his heavy mackinaw and plunged through the snow to join them. It was worth being suspended from his job to have time to play for a change.

Rissa waved to him. When she turned her back to work on the snowman, he scooped up a handful of wet snow and molded it into a tight ball. When he got closer to her, he said, "Hey, Rissa."

She turned and he threw the snowball at her, but she was quicker than he anticipated. She reached out her hand, caught the ball and tossed it back at him. It exploded in his face. All three of the sisters tackled him and rolled him over and over in the snow.

Laughing, he pushed them away and jumped to safety. "Just for that, I won't help you build a snowman."

Ignoring her sisters' surprise, Rissa put her arms around Drew's waist. "We're sorry. But you should know when you attack one Blanchard, you have to deal with all of us."

"That's what I'm afraid of," he said teasingly. Holding her tightly, he reached down, scooped up a handful of snow and rubbed it in her face.

"Well!" Juliet said. "Is there a romance going on right under our noses and we haven't even noticed? What have you guys got to tell us?"

"Not a thing," Rissa said. She grabbed Drew's hand. "Help us roll another ball of snow. We want a big snowman."

"The sun is supposed to be shining tomorrow, so he won't last long."

"Yes, but we'll have had the fun of making it."

They played in the snow for another hour until Drew said he had to leave. He had only come to be sure they didn't need anything. In spite of the snowplow, the roads were still treacherous and he didn't want to travel on the narrow road out of the Blanchard estate after dark.

Portia and Juliet started toward the house first and Drew pulled Rissa behind the large snowman and kissed her.

"Call me tomorrow when you can," he whispered.

* * *

Insolent eyes watched the foursome as they frolicked in the snow as if they were children without a care in the world. Bothersome brats! Had they forgotten so quickly that death had visited Blanchard Manor? Did they believe their troubles were over?

SIXTEEN

Rissa returned to the house, feeling warm and cozy after Drew's kiss. Soon she would be going back to the city to immerse herself in work, waiting impatiently for Drew to come for her. She had actually forgotten the cloud hanging over Blanchard Manor until she climbed the steps.

Juliet and Portia were sitting on the steps leading up to the third floor and they motioned frantically for her to join them.

"What's going on?" she whispered.

"We just got here. Listen," Portia said.

"Listen to me, old man," a woman shouted angrily, and it took Rissa a few moments to recognize the speaker as Sonya Garcia.

"She has her nerve to talk to Grandfather like that!" Rissa said.

Juliet, who had reason to be skeptical about Blanchard men, said, "Listen a little longer. We've heard enough to know that Sonya hasn't always been the meek, plodding housekeeper that we know."

"She said that Grandfather was glad enough to have her around when she had first moved to Blanchard Manor, but when she'd gotten old, he had shoved her away," Portia revealed.

"I think you owe me something," Sonya said. "You were glad enough to have me around at one time. But now you have no use for me and I'm working like a slave in this house, second in command to that Frenchman who rules the kitchen."

"This sounds like a one-way conversation to me," Rissa said. "Have you heard Grandfather say anything?"

"Not a word," Portia replied.

Remembering the day she'd talked about her clinical depression to her grandfather, when he'd been totally unresponsive, she doubted that he was even aware of what Sonya was saying. But regardless of what her grandfather had done in the past, she wasn't going to stand around and have him harassed.

"I'm going up."

"No," Portia said. "Sonya might be the one who's been committing these crimes, and she might kill you."

"Has it ever occurred to you that she might kill Grandfather? I'm going up," she repeated.

It had gotten too quiet on the third floor to suit her, and Rissa rushed upstairs and opened the door into her grandfather's room without knocking. Howard sat in his chair as usual. Sonya stood beside him, leaning over the table that held the tea things. She was pouring water in his teacup through tea leaves in a strainer, preparing his tea as she did each evening.

Howard sat with his eyes open. Peg Henderson wasn't in sight.

Sonya stared at Rissa and her two sisters, who stood in the doorway peering in.

"Good evening," Sonya said, her face as expressionless as usual.

"We heard shouting," Rissa said. "Is anything wrong?"

"Nothing at all, miss. Sometimes I have to shout to waken Mr. Blanchard."

Rissa turned and exchanged incredulous glances with her sisters. She walked farther into the room.

"Grandfather," she said, "I'm going back to the city soon. I wanted to say goodbye."

He smiled feebly and lifted his hand. Normally, Rissa would have kissed his hand, but after the revolting one-way conversation she had heard between Sonya and him, the love she had always felt for her grandfather crumbled around the edges. She took his hand and squeezed it slightly and turned away from him. *Why couldn't she have one pleasant memory of her father or grandfather to cherish?*

The next morning, the phone rang before Drew finished a breakfast of pancakes, sausage and coffee.

"Good news," Mick said. "The chief has decided to reinstate you until the board has time to review your case, which may not be for several weeks."

"Why this change of heart?"

"He's always been on your side in the matter," Mick said, "but he had to satisfy the politicians who watch every move he makes. Besides, we need you. There are some new developments in the Blanchard case. When can you come to headquarters?"

"As soon as I finish this last bite of pancake and take another swig of coffee."

"I'll fill you in when you get here."

It felt good to walk into headquarters in his uniform and to be given his badge and gun.

"So what's going on?" he asked Mick when he motioned for Drew to follow him into their joint office.

"We may have been suspecting the wrong people in the Blanchard case. You remember those pills you found at the scene of the crime when Trudy Blanchard was murdered?"

"Yeah."

"We've traced them to Howard—it's one of the medicines he takes. We learned that from the pharmacist."

Drew whistled sharply. "That would lead to a dead end. You can't question or convict a senile man."

Mick agreed with a nod. "According to Portia, her grandfather has always hated his daughter-in-law, and he's still mobile. Peg Henderson watches him diligently, but occasionally he gets away from her. There are also times when he's lucid. If I can catch him on one of those times, I'll question him. And I convinced the chief that you were the one to back me up."

"I'll do what I can, but it seems like a useless task."

"Also, that hitman still denies any knowledge of the Blanchard crimes, although he told one of the deputies that we were barking up the wrong tree. I went in and pounced on him about it, asking him how he knew anything about the case if he didn't know the Blanchards. He said he didn't know the family, but that there has been a lot of talk floating around town that Trudy's murder was an inside job by someone close to the family. If that's true, it could also point to Howard."

"I hope that isn't true. The girls harbor deep-seated animosity toward their father, but as I understand it, although Howard might be a scoundrel, he loved his granddaughters and they adore him."

Mick nodded agreement. "Will you go with me to talk to him?"

"Of course. It feels good to be back in the saddle again."

"And another thing…" Mick said as they prepared to leave the room.

"What now? You've already told me enough to ruin my day."

"You remember the key chain you found after Ronald had a confrontation with somebody in the gazebo? I thought there were probably millions of them sold around the world, but it seems that particular chain is made in California and is sold only in that state."

Drew whistled again. "Wow! That limits the field. How many people connected to this case have been in California recently?"

"Portia told me that Juliet had gone to California searching for her mother. Trudy Blanchard had been there before that, contacting an old lover of hers, Arthur Sinclair, who happens to be Juliet's father."

Drew pounded his forehead with the palm of his hand. "How many more skeletons are going to pop out of the Blanchard family closet? So both Juliet and her mother were in California?"

"Yes, as well as Brandon De Witte, Juliet's boyfriend. So that makes three people who could have dropped that key chain."

"But just because the woman in the gazebo dropped that key chain doesn't mean that she murdered anyone."

"I know," Mick agreed hopelessly. "This may be another dead end that leads nowhere."

After hearing the things Sonya had said to her grandfather the night before, Rissa hadn't called Drew, for she felt sure he would suspect she was upset about something. And the raw hurt in her heart kept her from wanting to talk to anyone, but she was disappointed when she tried to call him early the next morning and he didn't answer. Later when she looked out the window and saw Mick and Drew exiting a cruiser, she ran downstairs to open the door for them.

She had dressed for the day in a green cashmere body suit with a V-neck and bat-wing sleeves. Drew figured that the outfit probably cost a bundle, and she looked terrific. He wanted to hug her, but he was new at this relationship stuff, and he wasn't yet ready to make a public display of his affections.

Rissa swept questioning eyes over his uniform and holstered gun, and he said mockingly, "They found out they couldn't run the Stoneley police station without me. After they begged on bended knee, I agreed to come back and bail them out."

Mick groaned. "Give me a break!"

"Is anything wrong?" Rissa asked.

"Not that we know of," Drew said, wondering how much to tell her.

Mick held up the small vial containing the two pills Drew had found in the library on the night of the murder.

"These were found in the library on the night your mother was killed. It's one of your grandfather's prescriptions. We want to talk to him."

Rissa held up a hand. "Oh, please don't do that. You know his condition. It would upset him terribly."

"That may be true, but we have new evidence pointing to the possibility that the murderer is a member of the family. We've got to follow up every lead," Mick said resolutely. He started toward the stairs. "Is his door locked?"

"Not during the daytime. After Grandfather got away from Peg and crashed Aunt Winnie's birthday party, she locks the doors at night. She's good at watching him, but she has to sleep sometime."

Mick started upstairs, and Rissa cast a despairing look at Drew.

"It'll be all right. We'll be kind to him," he reassured her.

Drew followed Mick, and Rissa trailed them. Drew thought it would be best if she didn't sit in on the interview, but he understood her concern for her grandfather. He held out his hand and she gratefully slipped her hand into his. They couldn't do any more than forbid her to enter the room. Mick knocked forcibly on the door to Howard's apartment, and it opened slightly. Peg peered out.

"Why, what on earth!" she exclaimed, shocked. "What do you want?"

"We need to talk to Mr. Blanchard for a minute," Mick said.

An exasperated look spread across Peg's face, and she swung open the door. Howard was slumped in his chair, his head on his chin, saliva dribbling from his mouth as he slept.

"Help yourselves."

Peg evidently thought the sight of Howard's helpless state would deter them. But when the two officers stepped inside the room, she rushed after them like a fluttering hen defending her chicks.

"Don't you dare!" she snapped, her eyes flashing. This was a side to the nurse that Rissa hadn't seen before. But it was good for the Blanchard family that Peg took her role as Howard's guardian seriously.

Mick pulled a chair close to Howard. "Bring a cold cloth and wash his face," he said to Peg.

"I won't do it. I'll call the law on you."

"We *are* the law," Mick said, a glint of humor in his eyes.

"You get a cold cloth, Rissa," he said.

Rissa looked at Drew and when he nodded assent, she skedaddled into the bathroom. She brought a damp washcloth and tenderly wiped her grandfather's face.

"Why are you doing this?" Peg demanded, hovering over Howard.

"Because I intend to question everyone who has a motive to kill Trudy Blanchard. As soon as you let us find out what we can from Mr. Blanchard, we'll leave and let your patient alone."

When she tried to push Mick away from Howard, he caught her hand. "Miss Henderson, be reasonable. We mean no harm to Mr. Blanchard. I don't think you want to be cited for obstructing justice, which I'll do if you don't behave. The sooner you step aside, the faster we can complete this interview."

Frowning, the nurse jerked her arm out of Mick's grasp, but she still kept her hand on Howard's shoulder. "I'm not leaving the room."

Ignoring her, Mick said, "Mr. Blanchard, I want to talk to you about your daughter-in-law, Trudy."

Howard muttered and stirred in his chair, and Mick cast a significant glance in Drew's direction. Drew wondered just how sound asleep the man had been. Maybe he *was* guilty and he was just pretending to be asleep. This was Drew's first sight of the Blanchard patriarch, and when Howard opened his eyes and straightened in the chair, Drew was surprised at the strong personality of the man. Drew could understand why Howard Blanchard at one time had dominated the business world around Stoneley. He looked weak, but on occasion, could he exert enough physical strength to throw Rissa over the cliff?

"We need to ask you some questions, Mr. Blanchard," Mick said.

Howard stared at him, and his blank eyes drifted to Rissa and Drew.

"Do you remember your sister-in-law?"

Hatred shone in the man's eyes, so he must have understood Mick's question, but he didn't respond. This reaction caused Drew to question if Howard could understand what was said but didn't have the verbal skills to reply.

"Evil!" Howard muttered.

"You mean your daughter-in-law was evil?" Mick persisted.

Howard nodded his head vehemently.

"How long has it been since you've seen her?"

Howard shook his head.

"Have you seen her in the past few weeks?"

Peg stepped forward. "That *is* enough. I'm going to call his son. You have no right to persecute this man."

Mick nodded to Drew, who stepped toward Peg purposefully and she retreated. "Stop interfering or leave the room," he ordered.

Reluctantly, she moved farther away, and Drew stood where he could keep her from communicating with Howard.

"Do you know your daughter-in-law, Trudy Blanchard, is dead?"

The information seemed to startle Howard at first. Then, rocking back and forth in his chair, he laughed like a lunatic.

"Dead, is she?" he shouted gleefully. "Dead! She was evil and got what was coming to her. Whoever murdered her did the Blanchards a favor."

"How do you know she was murdered?" Mick said, but if Howard heard him, he didn't answer. He had slipped back into that silent world of his that no one could penetrate. His eyes were blank and lifeless.

Shrugging his shoulders, Mick stood up and motioned for Drew and Rissa to follow him. Peg hurried to her patient and hovered over him with deep concern. They walked silently downstairs and Rissa followed the two detectives out on the porch, wishing she knew how much evidence they had against her grandfather.

"Call me tonight," Drew said to Rissa, squeezing her hand.

He slid behind the wheel of the cruiser and waved to her. They cleared the gate of Blanchard Manor and Drew exhaled deeply as if he'd been holding his breath.

"It's no wonder to me that Rissa has clinical depression," he said. "That house is one of the most oppressive places I've ever been. I consider myself as levelheaded as any ordinary man, but when I'm inside Blanchard Manor, it seems as if evil is lurking in every corner. I have to constantly suppress the urge to peer over my shoulder to see what's behind me."

Mick nodded his agreement. "All of the sisters would be lunatics by now if they hadn't had the wisdom to leave home as soon as they could. The ones who went to boarding school and from there into college didn't live in the house for too long. Even at that, most of them carry scars they can lay at the feet of their parents."

"I know that Rissa does. When I think about what they've gone through, it makes me furious."

"According to Portia, Miranda is probably the worst emotionally. She has a bad case of agoraphobia—they can hardly get her to leave the house. I'm surprised she went to her mother's funeral."

"Winnie seems to be well adjusted," Drew said, and he slowed the cruiser as they entered Stoneley.

"Yes, and the girls owe a lot to her. However, her father broke up her youthful romance with Tate Connolly, and I wonder if she's ever forgiven him."

"So now Howard is the prime suspect for the murder of Trudy?"

"As far as I can tell," Mick speculated. "He had motive and opportunity. Those two pills you found are his sleeping medication. Let's suppose that Peg gave him the medication and he slipped it into his pocket. He could have sneaked out of the apartment after she went to her bed thinking he'd had enough dope to keep him immobile until morning."

"I watched him closely while you were questioning him, and I've decided that he's a lot more alert than anyone suspects," Drew said. "Because people think he's senile, they talk about issues in front of him, thinking he doesn't understand, so he knows more about what's going on in the household than anyone thinks he does. He may have refused his medicine more than once and wandered around the house at night."

"From his outburst today, I believe that he would have killed Trudy without any remorse, but what about the attack on Rissa? Surely he wouldn't harm her. According to Portia, Howard has always doted on the twins."

"Have you ever wondered if we might have more than one perpetrator in this situation?" Drew asked.

He felt Mick's sharp eyes piercing the distance between them. "Do you think the attack on Rissa could have been a copycat crime?"

"It's possible," Drew said as he swung into the parking lot at headquarters. They entered the building and went into their office. He reached for the notebook in his pocket. "Let's see where we stand now. The last time we talked, I made a list of our suspects. The last few days I've scratched off a few of those names."

"Let's hear who you've eliminated."

"Rissa, definitely! Alannah Stafford, Winnie and Barbara Sanchez. I'm discounting those because we don't have a speck of evidence to connect them to this crime," Drew explained.

"I'll go along with those with the exception of the Stafford woman. From what I've heard, she gets what she wants one way or another—and it's obvious she wants Ronald Blanchard, although for the life of me, I don't understand why."

Drew laughed at him. "That's because you're a man. It's women who fall for his handsome good looks and the suave manners he exhibits when he wants to. Now for the ones still on the list of suspects...."

"I think the hitman, Conrad Keefer, is lying. Let's keep him on the list. I was hoping he would crack before he went back to prison. The state police hauled him away this morning, still insisting that he didn't know anything about the Blanchard case."

"As far as I'm concerned, it's a toss-up between Ronald and his father for the murder of Trudy," Drew said as he made notes about the hitman in his notebook. "But I can't believe either one of them would hurt Rissa."

"I agree. So if one of the Blanchard men killed Trudy, we definitely have more than one perpetrator in this situation."

"But the only reason anyone would have to kill Rissa is to keep her from revealing what she saw in the library," Drew countered. "And as much as I dislike Ronald Blanchard, I don't believe he killed his wife."

Mick ran his hands through his hair and groaned. "So we're back to square one—only one murderer."

The phone rang and Drew answered. He listened intently and slammed down the receiver without saying a word. "Scratch Conrad Keefer. He escaped on his way to prison this morning," he muttered, disappointment ringing in his voice.

"So that leaves us with the Blanchard men. Which one do you think is the culprit?"

"Howard," Mick said.

"Okay. Then let's concentrate on him for a few days."

"Why don't you take the rest of the day off?" Mick suggested.

"I will, but I'll spell you at midnight."

Drew walked toward his cruiser, knowing that the time had come to make a definite move in his relationship with Rissa. He supposed that it was natural for him to be concerned about the differences in their social standing, but that hadn't kept Mick and Portia from becoming engaged. And he didn't intend to let that problem keep Rissa and him apart.

It was time for him to concentrate on what Rissa and he had in common rather than dwell on their differences. Having a family wasn't an issue for either of them. They both wanted to live in a city, and they shared a firm belief in God's direction for their lives, which was probably the most unifying factor of all. He was ready to commit. Tonight he would learn how Rissa felt about sharing the future together.

SEVENTEEN

Drew opened the door of his house and received his usual scolding from Rudolph, who pranced from one side of his enclosure to the other, acting like an angry child. Drew unlocked the cage door, filled the water bowl and feed tray.

"Pout if you want to," he said, "but if you want any exercise you'd better take it while you can. I'm going to visit a special lady tonight."

"Squawk!"

After he'd showered, Drew called Rissa on her cell phone. "I'm off work until midnight. May I see you this evening?"

"Yes, of course."

"What time do you finish dinner?"

"Seven o'clock."

"I'll come out about that time, and maybe we can walk around the grounds. The snow has almost melted here. I'd like some time alone with you before you leave. There are too many people in the house to find any privacy."

"We still have quite a few slushy spots on the lawn. But we can go to the gazebo. We can be private there, and it's in sight of the house. I'll admit that I'm a little skittish about being outside at night. I wish we could walk along the bluffs, but I don't think I'll ever want to go there again."

"I'm not sure it's safe, anyway. The hitman escaped on his way to prison today. If he was after you, as I suspect, you'll have to be cautious. When are you leaving for New York?"

"In a day or two, if it's all right with the authorities."

"I think I can arrange that. I'll miss you, sweetheart, but I want you out of harm's way as soon as possible."

Rissa's pulse always quickened when he called her *sweetheart*. "I want to go, but I'm leaving so many unanswered questions behind. Who tried to kill me? And why? Who tried to gaslight me by putting those things in my room? Why could I hear the woman wailing when no one else could?"

"If you find the answers to those questions, be sure and let me know. Mick and I lie awake at night trying to figure out who is causing all of this trouble."

"And I'd like to know why my family has been targeted. But enough about that. I'll be counting the minutes until you get here."

Drew was smiling when he hung up. He walked to the sink to draw a glass of water.

Rudolph zoomed out of his cage and landed on Drew's head.

"Now look what you've done, you pesky bird. You've

messed up my hair." He swatted the bird lightly. Rudolph squawked and swiftly perched on the pantry door.

"You have about fifteen minutes before you have to go back in the cage."

Rudolph turned his head and eyed Drew with displeasure.

Drew dressed in a pair of brown slacks, a khaki polo shirt and a brown leather jacket. Before he left his bedroom, he lifted the lid on a small chest in a dresser drawer, picked up an item and looked at it for several minutes before he put it in his pocket.

When he entered the living room, Rudolph screeched from his perch inside the large cage. "Goodbye, goodbye."

Drew didn't want the parrot flying around the house when he was away, so he secured the lock, which he had installed soon after he'd started to harbor the bird. Until then Rudolph had occasionally let himself out of the cage and ransacked the house.

The bird was a nuisance, but it was pleasant to have something, even if it was a bird, to greet him when he entered an otherwise empty house.

Rissa waited for him in the foyer wearing a gray fleece cape over the dress she'd worn to dinner. She stepped out on the porch when he parked in the circular driveway and snuggled into his open arms. He kissed her forehead and released her.

Dusk had settled around the mansion, a cool breeze wafted in from the ocean and a sliver of new moon hung over the bay. Without speaking, hand in hand they wandered to the gazebo.

As they climbed the steps, Rissa fleetingly recalled the altercation that had occurred here between her father and an unknown woman. Had Ronald met her mother in the gazebo, threatened her and subsequently lured her into the house to murder her? She shuddered, and Drew must have felt it, because he put his arm around her waist.

"Tonight, I'd rather not talk about the crimes that have plagued your family for the past few months. Let's think about pleasant things for a change. I want to talk about *us*."

"We do need to talk," she said. "I've decided to leave tomorrow afternoon and go back to New York. Aunt Winnie and my sisters, except Bianca, are having a fit about it. Bianca is leaving tomorrow, too. Delia has already gone back to Hawaii. I haven't mentioned it to Father—I'll tell him in the morning."

"Our relationship has been a strange one, interwoven with all this crime and mystery. But in spite of all the counts against us, it seems right for us to be together. Despite everything, I love you and want to marry you."

"That's what I want more than anything else," she murmured as he pulled her close and kissed her.

When their lips parted, Rissa said breathlessly, "I think we have a lot in common. I can't help where I was born any more than you can change your childhood. If I understand marriage, two different people become one, and our relationship from then on is what counts."

"That's a wonderful way to describe it. That's what comes of writing for a living, I suppose—being able to speak what you feel. Although I have very little conception of what your life is, I want to share it. Mick wanted

Portia to leave the city and come back to Stoneley, but I don't expect that of you."

"I don't think I could ever live in Maine again, although I'd try it if that's what you wanted to do."

He shook his head. "That won't be necessary. I'm sure I can get a job on a police force near you. Law enforcement is my life and I don't want to change that. But as crazy as it sounds, I believe we can be happy combining the lives of a playwright and a cop."

Rissa laughed. "I'll admit that putting it into plain words like that does make it seem impossible. But love will find the way to work out our differences."

"I wouldn't feel right to skip out on Mick and the others when they're in the midst of the most notorious crime wave of the town's history, so I won't resign yet."

"But you will come to visit me, won't you? We need some time together away from Blanchard Manor."

"Wild horses couldn't keep me away. And we'll be together when Mick and Portia have their wedding, although that's on hold, too, until the mystery is cleared up."

"I haven't even discussed it with Portia, but I don't think they'll get married soon. I've been thinking about where we will live. I rent an apartment but I don't know if you'd be happy there. It's plenty big enough. There are two bedrooms, besides a small room that I use for my office. You could use Portia's bedroom for your workroom. The living room and kitchen area are combined. I do have one question though. What about Rudolph?"

He grinned. "Rudolph isn't a city bird. When I leave

for New York, I'll find another home for him. I've only kept him now because I felt sorry for the bird when he lost his owner. Besides, I like to have somebody to talk to at night. But before too long I expect you to be waiting for me when I come home." He leaned close to her and his breath softly brushed her face.

Her heart danced with excitement and her voice trembled as she spoke. "That's a load off my mind. I'm not sure our relationship would survive if I had to compete with that bird for your attention."

"So you're willing to become officially engaged?"

"We can consider ourselves engaged but I'm not necessarily ready to make it public yet. And don't think I'm ashamed to have the family know that I'm engaged to you, but our love is so special that I'd just like for us to nurture it together before others get involved. And if it doesn't matter to you, I don't want a big wedding. Let's elope."

"Nothing could make me happier. I'd like that event to be special for us and no one else. I hope that isn't being selfish." He took a box out of his pocket. "I knew we wouldn't have time to choose a diamond ring before you left for New York—we can do that when I visit you. But I didn't want you to leave without a token of our engagement."

"Why, Drew, how sweet! I've been wondering if you were the romantic type, but I believe that you are."

"I don't know if I'll be romantic, either, but as much as I love you, I figure I will be."

He held the small box in his hand, wondering if she would laugh at such a simple token of his love for her.

"There's never been much money in our family, but I have a family antique that's been handed down through the generations, and I want you to have it as a reminder of our upcoming wedding." He gazed tenderly into her eyes. "One of my ancestors went to the California goldfields in the nineteenth century, and he brought home a special ring for his wife. It's passed from generation to generation, and before my father left home, he gave it to me."

He lifted a ring from the box and turned on the small flashlight on his key chain, showing a gleaming, wide-band ring. "The ring itself is made of gold and the stone is a piece of deep red coral. The initial *L* is etched underneath the band. It's never been resized. If it didn't fit, I guess the woman wore it on a chain. I know it doesn't compare with the Blanchard jewels," he said humbly, "but I'm offering it along with myself and my love."

Tears blinded Rissa's eyes and choked her voice. He held out the ring to her. It looked as if it would be a close fit, and she extended her left hand for Drew to place the ring on her finger.

He lifted her hand reverently and pushed the ring on her third finger. The fit was near perfect. He turned her hand and kissed the palm.

Smiling he said, "Grandpa always said that no Lancaster ought to propose to a woman unless the ring would fit her 'weddin' finger.' Looks as if I've made the right choice."

Rissa relished his bit of humor. The few hours they'd shared hadn't been conducive to any light repartee, and she knew she would cherish this moment as she did the ring. He turned off the flashlight, and she held up her hand and turned it so the security lights on the lawn would focus on the stone. With a touch of sadness she remembered that Drew would never have a son to pass the ring to.

Perhaps he sensed what she was thinking because he said, "It hasn't always gone down from father to son—doesn't matter as long as it's given by a Lancaster who descended from the original owner. I've got lots of male cousins."

"And it doesn't really matter to you?"

"Not anymore. If I have you, that's all I want. In the past few days I've recognized more than ever that my life is in God's hands. If He wants me to have a son, I'll have one despite what a doctor told me. The future is in His hands."

Rissa snuggled in his arms, content. She didn't know how many days would pass before they could finally be together. Or if some member of her family might be implicated in the murders. But the future had always been a mystery. God had brought her and Drew together for a purpose, and the future was in His hands.

* * * * *

*Can a long-lost love help Delia Blanchard
learn more about the body in the library?
Find out in DEADLY PAYOFF
coming from Love Inspired Suspense in
May 2007.*

Dear Reader,

I'm completing *The Sound of Secrets* prior to the Easter season 2006, and since the book will be published during the 2007 Easter season, my thoughts have turned to the resurrection of our Lord.

As you read this book, I pray that you will dwell on the meaning of the resurrection. "Because He lives, I will live also."

And because most of the readers of this book will be women, I will concentrate on the women's role in the resurrection. Even though they were grieving, the women prepared spices to anoint Jesus' body. Because they sought relief from their sorrow by doing something tangible, they were the first to hear the joyous news that Jesus had risen. Often those who are most blessed are those who continue to serve in spite of personal difficulties.

Once they heard the news of the resurrection, they were told to go quickly and tell what had been revealed to them. They hurried to tell others that Jesus was alive. When the angel delivered the message, He had completed His errand—it was up to Jesus' earthly followers to spread the Good News to the rest of the world.

My writing ministry has provided an opportunity for me to witness to the power of the resurrected Lord in my life. I pray that the Christian message in this book will encourage you in your walk with the Lord.

Sincerely,

Irene B. Brand

QUESTIONS FOR DISCUSSION

1. The Blanchards were definitely a dysfunctional family. Discuss the various members of the family. What could each of them have done to promote harmony in the home? Does it seem strange that the six sisters enjoyed a good relationship in spite of the stressful living conditions?

2. Name dysfunctional families in the Bible. Refer to Genesis, chapter 21, 27–32. Are there any similarities between the biblical families and the Blanchards? Did Rissa set the right example for her family by trusting God to help her through her difficulties?

3. What has caused the breakdown of the family unit in today's world? Think of dysfunctional families whom you know. Is there any parallel between these families and the characters in *The Sound of Secrets?*

4. What help can the Bible give to those whose marriages are in crisis? What advice would you give?

5. Study the following passages in the New Testament—Ephesians 5:22 and 6:4. Ronald Blanchard expected to be the head of his household. In disobeying their father, did the sisters fail to carry out the biblical command to honor their father? Is the advice of the apostle Paul archaic? Or is it still a valid way to approach harmonious relationships in the home?

6. Rissa relied heavily on the Bible to guide her decisions. Do you find it hard to follow God's way when it isn't what you want to do?

7. When are you most content in your Christian faith—when you live the way you know God wants you to or when you're rebellious? Why do you think this?

8. Do you believe that Rissa and Drew's marriage will be successful? What compromises will Drew have to make to fit into Rissa's world? Rissa is an individualist. How will she react to having a man underfoot all the time?

9. Is it possible that the deceit of her grandfather and father have scarred Rissa's life so that she will never find true happiness? What advice would you give a friend in Rissa's situation?

10. Have you ever suffered from clinical depression? Did you seek medical help? Did God's Word and prayer also aid you in overcoming this problem? How?

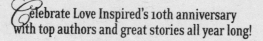